HONKYTONK BRAND

**Center Point
Large Print**

**This Large Print Book carries the
Seal of Approval of N.A.V.H.**

HONKYTONK BRAND

BRAND

WALKER A. TOMPKINS

CENTER POINT PUBLISHING

THORNDIKE, MAINE

This Center Point Large Print edition
is published in the year 2004 by arrangement with
Golden West Literary Agency.

The text of this Large Print edition is unabridged. In other
aspects, this book may vary from the original edition. Printed in
Thailand. Set in 16-point Times New Roman type.

ISBN 1-58547-506-8

Library of Congress Cataloging-in-Publication Data

Tompkins, Walker A.
    Honkytonk brand / Walker A. Tompkins.--Center Point large print ed.
        p. cm.
    ISBN 1-58547-506-8 (lib. bdg. : alk. paper)
    1. Large type books. I. Title.

PS3539.O3897H66 2004
813'.54--dc22

                                                            2004008723

ONE

While Big Yak was out at the barn saddling up for him, Wes Banning hustled into shirt and levis, cowboots and Stetson. He turned up the wick of the lantern to dispel the cabin's pre-dawn blackness and stood a moment debating whether to buckle on the Colt .45 which hung holstered on the shell belt hanging from a nail over his bunk. Then he elected to take the Winchester and lifted it from the antler rack over the fireplace.

He checked the loads in the magazine. "Steel jackets won't do it," he mused. "First shot's got to count. There won't be a second." He fished a soft-noser from a cartridge box on the mantel and thumbed it into the breech.

Outside he met Big Yak leading in the horse and he said "I'll eat when I get back with the pelt."

His Indian roustabout was skeptical, having argued that poisoned liver on a wolf trap was the only answer: "You go long time hungry, tillicum."

Banning mounted, retorting as he thrust the .30-.30 into the saddle boot, "You go to hell, you red-skinned fleabag," and put the sorrel through the solid dark at a jog-trot, spurring to a full gallop when they picked up the Circle B drift fence he and Big Yak had strung across the two-mile mouth of the Gap.

He forded Beaver Creek a good mile downstream from the willow-brake where the big cougar watered.

The chill kiss of the west wind, carrying the icy breath of the Cascade snowfields to his cheek, reassured Banning that the big cat would not scent him.

This cougar had been playing hell with fresh-dropped calves on Banning's leased graze. Five kills in the past seven nights, which was something a small-tally rancher couldn't afford very long. Big Yak, relying on his inherited savvy about such things, had tracked the varmint to its den in the talus under the South Rim. Neither of them had seen the predator by daylight.

Banning picketed his horse below the crest of a ridge which hid the South Rim from view of the ranch, and walked the remaining half a mile along the drift fence, carrying the carbine. The gray wash of the false dawn overtook him as he was reaching the motte of rhododendron scrub he had selected yesterday as his shooting blind. It was eight hundred yards to the talus where Big Yak said the cougar was laired, but the Winchester was true at that range and a soft-nose bullet would mushroom enough to rip the guts out of a bull elk.

He bellied down in the rhododendrons, stifling an impulse to smoke. Gradually the black skyline to the east began to swell and shimmer like the surface of a kettle of pitch fixing to boil. Suddenly the sun's blinding disk cut out from under the desert and the cliffs forming the south wall of Chinook Gap changed at once from indigo to blood red, throwing the vast slope of brush-dotted boulders along the base into sharp relief.

And there was the cougar, the biggest devil he had seen since coming to Washington Territory.

It was slinking languorously through the sagebrush toward the talus, its tawny hide blending perfectly with the rocky background but its elongated shadow giving it away.

Banning cocked the rifle, excitement bubbling through him. He made his allowances for elevation and windage. Over the sights he saw that the cougar was carrying the bloody carcass of a fresh-killed calf in its jaws. On her way to the den where hungry cubs were waiting, to hole up until nightfall and another raid on the Circle B herd.

With infinite care Banning estimated his range and his finger slid through the trigger guard, preparatory to squeezing off his shot. It was an alien sound somewhere behind him—the whicker of a horse—that broke the spell of Banning's concentration.

He took a quick glance over his shoulder, and promptly the cougar was forgotten.

A lone rider sat his horse a hundred yards away, on the opposite side of the barbed wire fence. At this moment the stranger was leaning from stirrups, the day's first sunrays striking a glint off a shiny tool in his gloved hand.

Banning heard a twanging sound transmitted along the taut-strung wire, saw the top strand give way before the bite of the horseman's pliers.

"A Butcherblock son, cutting my fence—"

The Circle B boss eased down the hammer of his

Winchester and came to his feet, his six feet four enabling him to stare over the rhododendrons. The chapclad rider dismounted now and appeared to be studying the north skyline of the ridge in the direction of Banning's ranch buildings, under the North Rim.

Satisfied that he was unobserved, the rider clipped the remaining three strands of barbed wire and then put his pincers into a saddlebag. Mounting, he backed his buckskin gelding off a few yards, untied a coil of lass'-rope from his pommel, shook out a loop and flipped it over the nearest fence post.

Then, as Banning watched in mounting anger, he saw the interloper dally his rope to saddle horn and begin spurring his pony back and forth in short arcs, all its weight on the rope. A moment later the pine post uprooted, letting another fourteen-foot barrier of wire collapse to the bunch-grass.

"One of Costaine's hard cases, I'll bet my last blue chip on that," Banning ground out. "I got this cougar hunt to thank for catchin' the son red-handed."

Banning raised his rifle and laid a shot into the rubble to spray the buckskin's brisket just as the rider was recoiling his rope before moving to the next post. By the time he got his horse under control again Banning had cut the distance between them to half.

For a moment he thought the Butcherblock cowhand was going to reach for his own carbine, booted under his saddle fender with the stock carried forward, owl-hoot style. Then, as if sensing that the odds were against his getting the piece into the clear in time, the fence-cutter hooked one knee over the pommel and relaxed in a stoop-shouldered posture, rolling a smoke.

It was a studiedly casual bit of business, intended to keep his hands well away from his six-gun stocks, but at the same time show Banning his contempt for the bad turn the situation had taken.

Something akin to fear twisted Banning's innards as he slogged along the sagging fence with chopping, long-legged strides. Not fear for the outcome of this meeting; his rifle was in command of this scene. It was fear of what this leering, arrogant fence-buster represented; he might be a harbinger of trouble that would be too steep for a lone cowman to buck.

There was a Butcherblock brand on the buckskin, Banning saw as he drew closer, confirming the fact that the fence-cutter was drawing Greg Costaine's pay. Something in the well-feigned carelessness of the man's demeanor as he lazily cemented his cigarette with a swipe of his tongue reminded Banning of the warning that Paul Priggee, the federal land agent, had given him over in Coulee Center two years ago when he had filed on the section of land comprising the north half of the Gap's entrance:

"No man by himself can buck a solidly entrenched combine like Butcherblock, son, not if he stays inside the law. Some have tried it before you and you'll find their graves up in the foothills. With the whole Territory to pick over, why file on grass that Costaine will be after sooner or later? It's like building a sand house on a beach in front of an ocean wave—"

Banning had shrugged off that warning, two years ago. He was twenty-eight then, born of pioneer stock that had fought for what they wanted as the frontier pushed westward from Kentucky.

A former Butcherblock cowhand, he had gone ahead and proved up on his section, with only his Indian roustabout to help him. Greg Costaine's vast Butcherblock empire had started from nothing larger than Circle B, under the regulations of the same Donation Land Act. Now Butcherblock cattle ranged over a stretch of country larger than some Eastern states, from a nucleus of Texas cattle that Banning had helped haze over the Bitterroots from Montana when he was a whiskerless kid of eighteen.

He had built his house. Whether he had built of transient material would soon be put to the test. The overwhelming ocean wave Priggee had predicted was here in the shape of this gunhung troublemaker forking a Costaine horse.

This rider wouldn't be Costaine, of course. Costaine supervised his sprawling leagues of cattle land from his citadel on Smoky Butte, a dozen miles south of Medicine Lodge. The bulk of Costaine's crews were gunswift hard cases imported from Texas. This wire-cutting hombre was probably one of them.

"Howdy," greeted the stranger, as Banning halted a dozen paces away, beside the fallen fence post. "You sure as hell git up early in the mornin' to hunt for trouble, don't you?"

Banning's rifle muzzle came to a level pointing, hip high.

"Start talkin'," the Circle B man said grimly, pure death in his metal-blue eyes. "What's your name and who ordered you to chop down another man's fence?"

TWO

The rider shrugged indolently, fishing in the pockets of his bullhide chaps for a match. He was a weasel-faced specimen, skin burned black as a Comanche's by sun and wind, his jowls blue with a growth of curly beard. Banning couldn't remember having seen him around Butcherblock when he worked for the brand.

His holsters, Banning noted, were not thonged down at the tips. They were fastened to his shell belts with big brass rivets which served as swivel pivots. A trick borrowed from the Mexicans, enabling a man to get off a shot without having to draw iron from leather. Not often seen this far north.

"The monicker's Tex Karnhizel. I was figgerin' to take a *pasear* up the Gap. You'll be Wes Banning?"

Banning scowled. Tex Karnhizel. Costaine must have something pretty hot on the fire to have dispatched his ace gunhawk up here on this fence-cutting deal. Karnhizel, so the range gossip went hereabouts, had left the border a couple of jumps ahead of a Ranger posse and had sought refuge on Costaine's payroll to avoid extradition. Butcherblock must be paving the way for something. Maybe, after all, it was that wave shaping up to roll in and engulf Circle B, as it had engulfed many another small-tally outfit that had bucked Costaine's combine in the past.

"I'm Wes Banning," the hard-bitten rancher

admitted. "You're welcome to pass through the Gap, even if it's under lease to me. But you got off on the wrong hoof, Karnhizel, not bothering to look up a gate in my fence. You'll find one on the far side of the creek, over the ridge yonder. Your short-cut is going to slow you down considerable this morning."

Karnhizel regarded Banning with a taunting insouciance while he lighted his cigarette. With his left hand, Banning observed. The other, spatulate fingers splayed out fanwise on a chap-clad knee, was only inches from a swivel holster.

Ejecting blue forks of smoke through his nostrils, Karnhizel gestured toward a mound of dirt a few yards away, topped by a weathered wooden post.

"I believe that bench mark is the south-east corner of the section you homesteaded, Senhor," Karnhizel drawled. "Which means you don't control the fence between here and the South Rim. So don't tell me to look up any gate."

Banning's mouth clamped in a tight roll against his teeth. He refused to let his glance shift toward the section corner post, knowing that if this gunman had been sent up by Costaine to kill him, he would have to keep his strict attention on the Texan's guns.

"This south section is part of the Gap, under lease to me from the Indian reserve," Banning said carefully. "I built the fence. You cut a hole in it. You're going to patch it up, Karnhizel. Beginning now."

The Butcherblock rider ignored the rifle leveled at his head. He folded his arms on his chest, slitted bottle-green eyes ranging off across the green bottom of Chinook Gap, which curved off and away toward the summit of the Cascade range.

"How many cattle you runnin' on this grass, Banning?"

"That's no business of yours, Tex, but if that's what Costaine sent you up to tally, you can tell him six hundred head and save yourself the trouble."

Karnhizel made a sniffing sound which carried all the scorn a big outfit held for a small-tally rancher.

"Accordin' to the government survey there's fifty-odd thousand acres in the Gap. Enough to graze ten thousand head."

Banning shook his head, anger needling him rashly.

"The way Costaine runs cows, yes. In Texas, you needed fifty acres to graze a single critter. Out here we figger ten acres to the head, allowing for bad winter years. Chinook Gap will handle five thousand cattle, no more. That's the herd I aim to build up."

Karnhizel flipped his half-smoked cigarette into the dust at Banning's feet.

"Costaine told me to scout the grass conditions in the Gap," he said indolently, "so I won't take up no more of your time, Banning. *Hasta la vis—*"

Karnhizel broke off in the middle of his Spanish idiom, reading the shoot signal in the whitening knuckle of Banning's trigger finger.

"You'll scout no grass of mine, Karnhizel. I reckon you carry staples and hammer in your saddlebags, along with your pincers. Get to work or I'll burn a cap on you."

13

Karnhizel's slanty eyes held no fear, only a deep-rooted sarcasm. He propped an elbow on his dish-shaped Brazos saddle horn and said in the gentle patronizing voice of an adult lecturing a wayward child,

"Listen, Banning. I'm savin' your bacon for you, only you don't know it. Right now, Chet Lattimer is rounding up twelve thousand head of Butcherblock feeders and she-stuff. You know who Lattimer is?"

"Costaine's foreman? I ought to. He fired me for objecting to Butcherblock's overgrazing good range, turning it into desert."

"That's right. Grass ain't so good this spring. So—"

"Because Costaine overstocked it for ten years."

"Makes no diff what the reason is," the gunman said waspishly. "What I'm tryin' to ram into that jug-head of yours is that Lattimer has got to shove that herd onto grass pronto or face a die-off. Costaine's picked out Chinook Gap here. Are you too thick between the horns to know a stacked deck when you see one?"

Banning's jaw trembled with curbed anger. Karn-hizel's words jolted him like a blow to the belly, because the gunman had spoken the blunt, unembroidered truth. Circle B *was* bucking a stacked deck. Costaine's ruthless methods of ranching had made him the cattle king of Washington Territory inside of ten years. There was talk that he aimed to sell out and throw his hat into the political ring next year, run for the Territorial Legislature from Foothill County, which he dominated.

A man like that wouldn't think twice about invading graze that was already under lease to another rancher. In a few months, twelve thousand head of stock could strip Chinook Gap naked, leave it open to complete ruin from winter erosion.

Red tape clogged the frontier courts so that it would take months to get an injunction against Butcherblock. Banning knew he could collect damages eventually; Uncle Sam would defend his prior right to the Gap. But an injunction would not restore the grass. Damages wouldn't insure Circle B's future prospects.

"I won't waste time arguing with a cheap tinhorn," Banning said hoarsely. "You got a post to set and some wire to string up. Unless Costaine has outfitted you with a bullet-proof hide, Tex, you better quit crowdin' my patience."

Karnhizel shrugged, then swung out of stirrups and went to work. Watching him reset the post, noting the sarcastic grin which carried no hint of anger in it, Banning knew what he was up against.

Karnhizel hadn't been sent here to murder him. His appearance as advance scout for the Butcherblock trail herd was intended to be a warning for him to pull stakes. Butcherblock was a cancer eating into the heart of the Territory's best grazing land, and as long as Costaine ruled Foothill County, no hand would be turned against him in his campaign to wipe out Circle B.

Twenty minutes later, when Karnhizel had finished repairing the fence and the two men faced each other across the barbed wire, Karnhizel paused for a parting word of advice.

"Where you made your mistake, son, was not gettin' yourself a pardner to prove up on this south section. That way you would control this end of the Gap, and the two of you would have had a legal right to keep the boss from hazin' his beef acrost it. As it stands, you're finished and don't know it."

Banning felt the sweet salt taste of blood on his tongue as his teeth wedged into his under lip, fighting back an immoderate impulse to gun this man down.

"Costaine uses his brains," Karnhizel went on, enjoying this slow torture he was inflicting on Banning. "Him and Chet Lattimer are ridin' over to Coulee tomorrow so Lattimer can file on this section next to yours. Not that Lattimer aims to bother provin' up on it. All the boss needs is a gate into your Gap, Banning. Soon as he visits the land office in Coulee he'll have it, and you'll be out-foxed forty ways from the deuce."

With which the Texas man mounted to wheel his gelding and sink in the hooks, heading southwest toward the rolling foothill country until he was lost to view beyond a ridge forming a knee of the South Rim.

Only then did Banning realize he still held his rifle ready for business against his thigh.

"You've talked too much, Karnhizel," Banning said aloud, his eyes still holding a stormy residue of passion. "You've tipped Costaine's hand, told me how to block him at his own game—"

Banning slogged back over the ridge at a run, and was limping by the time he reached the picketed sorrel.

16

Back at the ranch he found Big Yak waiting expectantly, disappointed not to see the big cougar's hide rolled up behind his boss's cantle.

The stolid-faced Yakima buck remained silent as Banning told him of Costaine's plan to invade his lease for summer graze.

"I'm heading for Coulee Center," Banning wound up. "I've got to file on that south section before Costaine beats me to it tomorrow. I figger by changing horses at Showalter's ranch and Anvil Ferry I can make it before Priggee's office closes tonight."

The Indian, knowing a little of the complications of land ownership under the palefaces' law, grunted skeptically: "You ketch one square mile of land, all gover'ment gives one man, unless he has squaw in his lodge. You ketch squaw in Coulee?"

Banning flushed, knowing what Big Yak was hinting at. Donna Fleming ran a dressmaking shop in Coulee, and she had promised to come to Circle B as Banning's wife when he had built himself a home fit for a wife. This sod-roofed cabin of squared logs wouldn't meet Donna's requirements by a damn sight, he knew that. But there was an alternative.

"Maybe not a squaw, Yak," Banning said gravely. "I figger Tom Romane will be willing to be my dummy pardner. Tom's always hankered to try home-steadin'."

Banning wolfed down the hot coffee and slabs of salt bacon Yak had prepared in his absence, and left the ranch twenty minutes later on a fresh horse, with Showalter's Lazy S ranch, forty miles distant, his first objective.

The sun was less than two hours high, thanks to the cougar hunt that had gotten him out of his bunk at three-thirty. The county seat was ninety miles away, but Banning figured he could reach Paul Priggee's office before it closed for the day, and have time to talk Tom Romane, his saddlemaker friend, into filing on the south section for him.

Ninety miles in eleven hours. Virtual desert, most of it, which ten years ago, when Banning had first seen it as a Butcherblock drover, had been belly-high to a bull with lush wild grass. Grass that Costaine's teeming herds had stripped to the roots, giving the snows and rains and winds their chance to scour the fertile volcanic topsoil into the Columbia River and on to the sea.

If he lost this race across the county today, Banning knew that two years from now the fertile Eden of Chinook Gap would revert to desert too, irrevocably denuded of forage. Circle B would be a vanished dream, and with his ranch Banning knew he would lose Donna Fleming as well . . .

THREE

Blood-red dusk overtook Wes Banning on the rimrock overlooking Coulee Center's ugly sprawl of shack roofs. He pulled his horse down to a walk, the third horse he had ridden from Circle B, knowing he had lost his race with the sun. Priggee closed his land office at five. It was now crowding seven-thirty.

The thought of marking time in this grubby cowtown

until tomorrow morning would have been intolerable had it not been that it gave him his first chance in better than three months to see Donna, to taste the warmth of her lips and feel her softness in his arms again.

Maybe it was for the best, getting slowed down when the bronc he had picked up at Showalter's had thrown a shoe after only six miles of riding, forcing him to ride back to Lazy S for a replacement to take him on to the Anvil Ferry stage station.

Getting in too late to do business today, he would have a chance to explain his dilemma to Donna, maybe argue her into a hasty wedding so that she could file on the south section first thing in the morning, before Costaine and Lattimer got in from Butcherblock headquarters at Smoky Butte.

He put the badly-winded roan stallion down the wagon road that had been blasted out of the coulee wall for stage traffic, his eye picking out the yellow false front of the Stockman's Bank where Donna had her upstairs dressmaking shop. Its windows were dark, but he knew that at this hour she would be having supper at the Elkhorn House where she had lived since the death of her parents.

Lights were beginning to blink here and there along the cross-hatched pattern of Coulee Center's streets when Banning reached the black archway of Cy Crowfant's Feed & Livery at the intersection of Columbia Road and Main Street.

Diagonally across Main, a barker stood on the awninged porch of Madam Bartreau's Paris Casino, thumping a bass drum and chanting an unintelligible sing-song designed to lure trade from the town's other deadfalls and honkies. A couple of white-jacketed housemen were propping ladders against the porch roof, getting ready to light the kerosene torches which projected over the street.

Old Cy Crowfant emerged from the livery barn as Banning stepped down from stirrups, stiff-jointed from his hellish relay race out of the foothill country. Limping on the leg that had caught a rebel minnie ball at Antietam, the old stable tender took the reins from Banning, his tongue making a dry click of disapproval as he noticed the horse's heaving flanks, the dust-muddied lather dripping from the saddle cinch.

"Man must be in hell's own hurry to buck the tiger and git hisself drunk, to mistreat hoss-flesh like this," Crowfant groused, not yet recognizing his customer. "Or would you be Paul Revere, come to warn us that the Siwashes are on the warpath?"

Just then the oil torches bloomed into flame from the long facade of Madam Bartreau's place and the guttering light gave Cy Crowfant his first look at the rider's fatigue-rutted face and stubbled jaw, cheeks burned to the color of oily bronze by the weather of the Cascade country.

"Oh—it's you," Crowfant apologized. "Spoke too quick, Wes. Mistook you for one of them hoss-killin' Butcherblock sports tryin' to show off. Reckon you got good reason for racin' your nag's hoofs down to the frawgs."

If Crowfant was fishing for information, he couldn't have heard Banning's explanation. The drummer on the Paris Casino's gallery was filling the gathering twilight with a tom-tomming cacophony that sounded like the pounding of an over-taxed heart, beating up echoes against the lava cliffs which hemmed the town.

The monotonous racket rubbed Banning's nerves and he shouted over the drumming, "Business so slack the Madam has to turn her brothel into a circus sideshow?"

He followed Crowfant into the ammoniac stench of the stable, where the noise was less objectionable. Crowfant put his horse into the first stall, stripped off and hung up the saddle, and reached for his curry comb and brushes.

"The Madam's been losin' trade to a bunch of fancy sportin' gals at the White Palace, so she's imported herself a singer from Montany to entice the boys back to the Casino."

As Banning was turning to leave he caught sight of a magnificent white Arabian stud further down the row of stalls. Sight of that horse and the silver-mounted saddle pegged on the wall behind it froze Banning in his tracks, a prescience of disaster running through him.

"That's Greg Costaine's hot-blood, ain't it?"

Crowfant peered at the Circle B man over the withers of the roan, sensing the despair that had prompted the query and half-guessing at what lay behind it.

"Reckon so, son. Him and his ramrod, Lattimer, breezed in from Medicine Lodge this evenin'."

"What time?" Banning's voice carried a sharp edge of suspense.

"Oh, five-thutty, guess 'twas. Mebbe later."

Relief flowed through Wes Banning, easing the tension that had made his tissues feel like over-wound clocksprings ever since his encounter with Tex Karnhizel up at the Gap this morning.

He thought, "They got here after the land office closed, then, which means the two of 'em will be roosting on Priggee's steps tomorrow. I wonder if Karnhizel deliberately gave me a wrong steer about when they were coming to town?"

He sensed Crowfant's eyes boring at him.

"Wes," the old hostler spoke hesitantly, "I don't know if you and Costaine have tangled, but there's somethin' you ought to know. Costaine was packin' two guns on his hip. Ain't seen him loaded like that for years. And it goes without sayin' he hired Lattimer for his gunslick more'n his cow savvy. If you rode over huntin' Costaine, you ought to know he's got his bodyguard with him, primed for trouble."

Banning said, "Thanks for the tip, Cy," and unconsciously touched the cedar butt of the Colt .45 holstered at his flank.

Crowfant, his rheumy eyes not missing that gesture, cut a paring of tobacco from his cut plug and tucked it between his molars, regarding Banning intently.

"Costaine's big, Wes, and he'll keep gettin' bigger until the whole Territory is under his heel like Foothill County is," the stable man prophesied gloomily. "I'm trustin' you to forgive me for talkin' to you liken as if

22

I was your daddy. You're thirty, ain't you? I could be your grand-pappy."

"What are you driving at, Cy?"

Crowfant coughed. "I just don't want to see Costaine rowel you into doing anything rash tonight, son. In case you had a run in with him and was lucky enough to smoke Lattimer out of the play, Sheriff Jeffers wears Costaine's collar and he'd see you hang. You're on the peck, if I smell gunsmoke aright, and I don't want to see you windin' up under a boothill mound afore you and Donna Fleming git your chance at double harness."

Banning's chill laugh floated back to the old hostler as the cowman headed for the stable door: "Don't worry yourself about what brought me to Coulee tonight, Cy. I'm here on the same business that brought Costaine in, which don't concern you."

Rebuffed, Crowfant went on with rubbing down the gelding. He had seen a lot of men die on the dusty streets of Coulee, and his spirit held a deep foreboding as he saw Wes Banning stalk out of the stable, dreading what this night portended.

FOUR

Quartering across Columbia Road, Banning debated about heading for the Elkhorn on the chance of joining Donna Fleming at supper, and decided against it. He needed a shave and a haircut. Donna was finicky about things like that.

The Red Saddle restaurant was directly opposite the stable and Banning turned toward it, aware for the first time of the hunger pangs in his belly. At the door of the cafe he paused to scan the red-painted canvas banner which Madam Bartreau had hung along the false front of her bagnio, illuminated by the glare of oil torches:

COME ONE, COME ALL!
PREMIERE PERFORMANCE OF
MADEMOISELLE MADELINE
THE MONTANA MEADOWLARK
Songs to Bring a Lump to Your Throat
and a Tear to Your Eye — the Loveliest
Chanteuse West of New York
SHE SINGS NIGHTLY AT
9 — 11 — 12 and 2 a.m.

Entering the restaurant, Banning took an obscure corner table, knowing he was not apt to run into Costaine at an eatery catering to mulewhackers and cowpunchers. No, Costaine would dine at the Elkhorn, as befitted the cattle baron he was. Anger stirred Banning as he realized that Costaine might be at Donna's table at this moment, charming her with his flattery and courtly fooferaw.

Meal finished, Banning visited a barber shop. He had made up his mind to drop in on Donna at the hotel tonight and tell her of his desperate situation at Chinook Gap, on the off-chance that she might give up her dreams of a fancy church wedding and help him gain possession of the south section. He would have to be at his best to swing her to his way of thinking, he knew.

Donna Fleming was a proud and beautiful girl and in his secret heart Banning had never been able to understand his luck at getting her to wear his engagement ring. Daughter of a Coulee City bank president, now dead, Donna was a prize in this raw and untamed land where single women were scarce, outside of a redlight house like the Paris Casino.

He had been working for Butcherblock for forty a month and beans when he had met Donna at a Christmas dance in the schoolhouse. He had known then that every eligible male in the foothills coveted her company. *Both Pagan (check it out yourself!)*

Nevertheless, the miracle had occurred. Donna had accepted his proposal the following Easter. That was three years ago. Without her inspiration, Banning knew he might still be punching cows for Costaine. It was Donna who had prodded him into filing on his homestead at Chinook Gap, prodded him into going into debt to Jim Showalter of the Lazy S to get stock enough to qualify for leasing the fine graze in the Gap from the Indian reservation.

He had come a long way in two years, thanks to Donna Fleming's ambitious nature and her faith in him. All that stood between him and Donna's hand in marriage was a home worthy for a woman to live in. But that took money, and he was still in debt for the cattle he had bought from Showalter as the start of his herd.

By the time he left the barber shop, Banning had changed his mind.

"Wouldn't be fair to ask Donna to move into that boar's nest that Big Yak and me built," he thought with bitter resignation. "Tom Romane's the answer. I can throw up a shack for him and when he gets a patent to the south section a year from now he'll sell it back to me. By then maybe I'll be in shape to bring a wife home and start a family."

He headed down street past the Paris Casino, ears wincing to the raucous braying of the Madam's drummer, and turned down Scabrock Road toward Tom Romane's harness shop and saddlery. Paul Priggee's land office was next door. He would spend the night in Tom's spare bunk so the two of them could be on hand bright and early tomorrow before Costaine and Lattimer showed up at Priggee's door.

It was shaving it pretty thin, but he knew Romane would cooperate with him in getting control of the south section and thereby throw a legal barrier between Butcherblock's herd and summer graze in Chinook Gap.

Romane's front door was padlocked, and when Banning got to the lean-to shanty in the rear where the saddlemaker lived, he was surprised to find it locked as well, the window dark.

Having come out from Montana with Romane, Banning knew Tom's habits. After suffering a heart attack during a round-up out on Butcherblock's range, Romane had come to town and opened up this harness shop and saddlery. Romane was a teetotaler and gambling was against his scruples, hence he never tasted

Coulee Center's night life. Thinking that his old friend might have turned in early, Banning knocked sharply on the door.

A window sash ran up across the alley and caught Banning in a fanwise spread of lamplight from the back end of the land office where Paul Priggee had his living quarters. Priggee's bald head was thrust out the window now and his greeting told Banning that the land agent did not recognize him:

"Lookin' for Tom Romane, feller?"

"Howdy, Paul. That's right. Figgered to drop in on you a little later, after I roundsided with Tom—"

Priggee pushed his reading glasses up on his forehead and squinted at the tall shape of the man across the alley.

"Well, if it ain't Wes Banning . . . Bein' lost out in the hills like you are, I guess you haven't heard about Tom."

"What?" Banning echoed, a cold premonition of tragedy growing in him at Priggee's inflection.

"I found Tom Romane dead in bed the other morning, Wes. Week ago yesterday, it was. Heart trouble. If'n I could have got word to you about the funeral—"

Banning's slumped posture showed the double shock of grief at his old friend's passing, and what Tom Romane's death meant to his own precarious future. Donna was his only chance now . . .

"Paul, if you got a minute, I'd like to talk with you—"

"Sure—always got time to talk with a friend, Wes."

27

The land agent ducked out of sight and a moment later ushered Banning into the lean-to. A huge map of Foothill County and the neighboring Indian reservation was tacked on one wall of the room, checkerboarded with township lines. Banning's attention went at once to that map as he shook Priggee's hand.

"Hate like hell to greet you with such melancholy news, first time in a coon's age that I've seen you, Wes," Priggee said, waving his visitor toward a chair. "Been wondering if Costaine had put pressure on you to sell out, but I haven't seen any transfer of title in the county records . . . Had supper?"

Ignoring the proffered chair, Banning walked over to the big chart and put a finger on his Circle B section.

"Costaine's in town tonight with the intention of filing on this section immediately south of me at the mouth of the Gap, Paul," Banning said. "In the name of his foreman. If he does, my prospects will be shot to hell."

Priggee settled himself in his ancient Morris chair and listened intently as Banning told his story, referring to Tom Romane only in reference to his blasted hopes of registering the south section in his friend's name.

"So Costaine has done what I told you he'd do," Priggee said when Banning finished. "He's turned his greedy eye toward the last patch of unspoiled range in this part of the Territory . . . Can't Miss Fleming prove up on this south section for you, son? The law allows a married man two contiguous homesteads. That would seal off the mouth of the Gap to Butcherblock."

Banning stared miserably at his friend.

"I aim to ask her," he said. "It's my only choice. But I'd rather be drug through Hell at the end of a lass'-rope than put the proposition to her, Paul. I ain't got much out there for a woman. This ain't the covered wagon days, you know!"

Paul Priggee's gnarled hands clasped together over an updrawn knee, horny thumbs rotating as he eyed Banning with a keen, probing sagacity.

"If Donna is a woman worthy of your love," he whispered gently, "she won't think twice about giving up the flashy trimming of a fancy weddin'."

Knots of muscle worked at the corners of Banning's jaws as he thought over Priggee's words.

"I'll go see her," he said heavily, "and lay my cards on the table. But it won't be easy."

Priggee accompanied Banning to the door. Standing there, he put a wizened hand on the younger man's shoulder.

"Tell you what I'll do, Wes," he said thoughtfully. "If Costaine is coming to see me in the morning, we got to work a sandy. I'll—I'll go so far as to transact the deal for you and Donna tonight, Wes, and date it on my books as having taken place prior to closing time this afternoon. It ain't legal by a damn' sight, and Uncle Sam's inspectors would crucify me for doing it, but if it'll help spike Costaine's guns and save Chinook Gap graze, I'm willing to take my chances."

FIVE

Banning averted his gaze, emotion choking him. He knew Priggee's iron-clad moral standards. Considering what was at stake, Priggee must be acting in the best interests of the Territory's future as well as doing a personal favor for a friend at the risk of his professional reputation.

"Donna and me could get the Baptist skypilot to marry us and show up at your office before midnight, Paul."

Priggee nodded. "I'll get the paper work taken care of," he said. "God bless you, son. The Territory could use more men like you . . . I'll wait up until you and Donna get here. I know she won't fail you, son."

Banning left the land agent's home and headed for Main Street and the Elkhorn House where his fiancée lived. It was after eight-thirty and Coulee Center's main stem was crowded at the corner in front of the Paris Casino, as the drummer's noisy harangue drew attention to the "Montana Meadowlark's" premiere performance, scheduled for nine.

Arriving at the hotel he found the lobby deserted. During the time he had courted Donna Fleming, he had never visited her in her upstairs suite, knowing the damage such an innocent meeting could do to a good woman's reputation in a cowtown such as this one.

But tonight the stakes were too desperately vital to them both to let convention stand in the way. He climbed the stairs to the upper floor and came to a halt in front of Room 7, where Donna had moved upon the death of her parents several years ago.

Lamplight glowed through the keyhole and he could hear Donna chatting inside, the liquid accents of her voice making his heart speed up and firing his blood with the hot hungers he had kept pent-up for so long a time.

Donna had company. Perhaps one of the town's housewives, come for a private fitting instead of at the dressmaking shop. That would be clumsy, but time was urgent tonight.

He poised his hand to knock, glancing up the dimly-lighted hall. Greg Costaine kept a suite of rooms in this hotel, for use on his infrequent trips to the county seat. It would not do for Costaine to know he was in Coulee Center tonight. The Butcherblock boss, knowing that Banning did his trading at Medicine Lodge and that Circle B's spring calf round-up would keep him too busy to visit the county seat merely to court Donna Fleming, might put two and two together and conclude that some land transaction was the reason back of his presence in Coulee.

In the act of rapping on the door of the girl's room, Banning's ears caught the deep-throated laughter of a man.

Anger flared quickly in Banning, anger with a flavor of jealousy in it. Then common sense told him that there would be some innocent explanation for his fiancée entertaining a man in her room, something Banning had never permitted himself to do. Maybe it

31

was old Zeke Brown, owner of the Elkhorn and a long-time friend of Donna's folks.

"Wish you'd reconsider it, Donna," the male voice reached Banning through the flimsy partition. "They say this girl is a regular prima donna. I think you'd enjoy the evening. The whole town will be there. It's not as if—"

"Donna Fleming inside a—a den of iniquity like the Paris Casino?" the girl interrupted her visitor. "Why, I'd lose every customer I've got. They'd say I wasn't respectable, Cecil."

Again that throaty laugh, followed by "Maybe you're not, Donna, letting a cardsharp like me kiss you. But don't you think it's possible to carry respectability too far? You—"

Banning waited to hear no more. He seized the knob and, finding the door bolted on the inside, smashed his shoulder against the panels with a force which broke the castiron mortise lock and sent the door swinging wide open.

Donna Fleming stood there with her hands lifted to rest on the shoulders of a tall, frock-coated man whom Banning recognized as Cecil DeWitt, a tinhorn employed by the White Palace saloon as a roulette croupier.

He would carry to his grave the picture that confronted him: Donna's shimmering wheat-blonde hair cascading to her shoulders, her seductively-curved body wrapped in a peach-pink quilted robe that opened to expose the cleft of her bosom.

DeWitt's slim, fishbelly-white hands were clasped

32

loosely behind Donna's back. Banning had the impression that the two of them, frozen there by the surprise of his entrance, had been clinging to each other in a more intimate embrace bare moments before.

Banning saw the quick fear cross DeWitt's pallid, handsome face, saw the pair break apart to face him guiltily, like lovers caught in a clandestine intimacy. The rancher's hands dropped, thumbs hooking inside his cartridge belt as he gave the pair the solid strike of his gunmetal eyes. He spoke in a dead monotone:

"Get out, DeWitt, before I kill you."

SIX

The gambler licked his lips, his teeth making their white flashing under his pomaded mustache. Banning was staring at Donna, reading the terror in her chalk-pale cheeks, the look of a trapped animal showing in amber eyes he had seen light up so often with love for him.

"Wes," Donna said in a frightened whisper, "don't go getting any ideas into that jealous head of yours. Mr. DeWitt lives down the hall and he just dropped in to see if I wanted to go—"

She broke off with a gasp as she saw Banning stride into the room. Pure terror had paralyzed DeWitt, seemingly; he remained rooted at his tracks, offering no resistance as the big range rider seized the collar of his fustian coat and the slack of his marseilles breeches and, literally lifting the gambler off the floor, propelled

33

him through the doorway and hurled him head over heels to crash heavily into the opposite wall of the corridor.

Banning closed the door on DeWitt's groaning shape and wheeled to face Donna Fleming.

"I well-nigh killed three horses to reach town tonight, Donna. I'll overlook finding you in that card-sharp's arms, knowing it's lonesome for you, wearing my ring and not seeing me for weeks on end—"

Donna sat down shakily on a horsehair divan facing him. Some color was returning to her cheeks now and he saw anger put its ugly strain on her lips.

"I'm in a jam at Circle B," Banning went on. "I need your help, Donna."

The girl finally found her voice. "You come charging into my room like a wild bull, you humiliate Mr. DeWitt in front of me as if you were a jealous schoolboy . . . and you still have the nerve to ask me to help you, Wes?"

Banning sucked in a breath to the pit of his lungs.

"Does DeWitt mean so much to you, Donna?"

She retorted angrily, "What do you want, Wes? Out with it."

He was silent for a long moment, telling himself how different this meeting was from what he had anticipated during the spine-pounding miles of his ride across Foothill County today. Her ripe lips were no longer inviting his love-making; they were locked in a down-curled line and her eyes carried a cold defiance that cut him to the core.

"Costaine aims to run twelve thousand feeders and

she-stuff into the Gap as soon as his spring round-up is finished, Donna," Banning heard himself saying dully. "The only way I can block him off is to file on the other section south of me and seal off the entrance to the Gap."

"And where do I fit into your schemes, Wes?"

He cuffed off his Stetson and stood staring at her, feeling a sick disillusion taking form inside him.

"I want you to marry me . . . tonight . . . so you can file on that section as my wife, Donna. As we have always planned to do."

Donna stood up, her fingers twisting at the small diamond on her left hand, in a gesture fraught with ghastly portent to Banning as he watched.

"You wouldn't have to live out there—just yet," he said hastily. "It's not—as cold-blooded as I made it sound, Donna. It's my only chance to fight Butcherblock."

She came toward him now, and he believed he had never seen her look more lovely, more desirable than she did in this moment, her willowy body sheathed in the satin robe that hugged the curves of her firm breasts and slim waist.

"You would use me to get title to more land, Wes? How little you know the ways of a girl's heart. How cheaply you must have held my love. Wes, I have been planning to write you. I am in love with . . . with Cecil DeWitt. I intend to marry him."

He was vaguely aware of her pressing the betrothal ring into the rope-calloused cup of his palm. She had

35

halted at arm's length from him, close enough for him to catch the heady aroma of the perfume she wore, an aroma that had taunted his dreams at night during the past two years of separation and struggle when his every waking hour had been devoted to building a foundation for the home and family that would one day be theirs. Now that dream was shattering before his eyes.

"If a woman is all it takes to fight Costaine," Donna Fleming taunted him, "why don't you try the Casino or the Palace? Those percentage girls are closer to your level than I will ever be."

He stood for a full minute, staring at the scorn in her eyes that he had never seen roused to anger before, loath to accept the reality of this disaster, wondering what a world would be like that did not have Donna Fleming as its reason for existing.

"So long, Donna," he said heavily, wheeling to stalk to the door, knowing he was walking out of her life forever. What little edge of his brain was still capable of rational thought told him that it was better this way, that Donna Fleming had never been meant for him.

Stepping out into the hall he saw Cecil DeWitt pulling himself shakily to his feet, eyes reptilian bright, his hand dabbing a handkerchief to his nose to stem its bleeding.

"She's all yours, tinhorn," Banning said with a breathy release of tension, and headed down the hall staircase and out of the Elkhorn like a man in the toils of a nightmare.

Reaching the street he tossed Donna's ring into the

dirt between the wooden curb and a hitchrack, recalling that it had taken four month's wages to buy the bauble from a Tacoma jeweler.

The solid cadence of the hawker's drum over on the porch of the Paris Casino assaulted his ears as he stalked down the plank sidewalk. It took some time for the drummer's spiel to filter into his numbed consciousness:

"The Montana Meadowlark's show is about to start inside, gents. The loveliest singer west of the Pecos. Don't miss the treat of a lifetime—the voice that has broken a thousand hearts—"

Donna Fleming's last taunt re-echoed in Banning's head as he approached the Paris Casino steps: *"If a woman is all it takes to fight Costaine, why don't you try the Casino percentage girls?"*

Something quite outside himself took control of Wes Banning in this instant. Hitching his gun belt, the Circle B rider crossed the saloon porch and shouldered through the batwing doors into the packed interior of the barroom.

SEVEN

The muted roar of the barroom throng was audible through the flimsy partitions of the dressing room where Becky Mullinary sat before the blemished looking glass, her hands trembling as she tried to mask the ravages of weeping with rouge pot and mascara.

Her being in this honkytonk, calling herself "Mademoiselle Madeline, the Montana Meadowlark," was so completely fantastic that her mind refused to tolerate the reality of the tawdry surroundings. The nightmarish events which had brought her to this saloon were enough to make her doubt her sanity.

Saloon was a very polite name for Madam Bartreau's establishment, she knew. Half of the downstairs section of the Paris Casino was given over to a dance hall, with a mahogany bar lining one wall. Beyond that was the big, smoky room where shaggy-bearded men gambled at the roulette wheels and poker tables, the faro layouts and chuckaluck cages.

Before this morning, Becky Mullinary had never set foot inside a public saloon, let alone this place of Madam Bartreau's. The Madam gleaned most of her sordid profits from the earnings of her so-called "dancing girls," who plied a more ancient profession in the cribs upstairs.

Applying paint to her full wide mouth, Becky Mullinary fought back the panic in her young body, telling herself over and over again, "Fifty dollars a week . . . three weeks will see me with enough money to get back to New York. Until I do this will be as good a hiding place as any . . ."

She felt contaminated by the tawdry surroundings of this dressing room, its racks filled with gay-colored gowns sparkling with tarnished sequins, the air smelling of stale perfume and cheap toilet water.

"They'll never trace me here," she told her reflection in the mirror. "That's all that matters now—"

The door at her back opened without the formality of

a knock, briefly admitting the pandemonium of noise from the crowded barroom—the profane roistering of men, the clatter of bottles on shot glasses, the brassy voices of the percentage girls she had met this evening—Straight-Edge Sal and Babe Rose, Fat Fifi and all the rest.

Becky stiffened as she caught sight of Madam Bartreau's porcine shape waddling toward her in the mirror, crooked snags of green-stained teeth grinning under the fuzz of mustache that downed her long upper lip.

"Dearie, it's five after nine and the boys are gettin' restless. You about finished with the primping?"

Becky stood up, hoping that Madam wouldn't guess the terror that rode her. When she had applied for the job at the Paris Casino this morning she had told Madam Bartreau she was a singer lately employed by the notorious Alder Gulch Palladium in Virginia City, Montana—a name she had picked at random from an advertisement in a mining journal she had found in the stage company's waiting room at Ellensburg two days ago. A ballad singer billed in the mining camps as the Montana Meadowlark. Madam Bartreau, hearing her sing, had hired her on the spot. She had even provided Becky's gown and garish jewelry.

"Y-Yes. I'm ready, Madam."

She turned from the dressing table to face the Casino's obscene, triple-chinned proprietress, mentally steeling herself from the lascivious eyes behind the greasy hammocks of flesh which ran over the curves of her trim figure, sheathed in a silver lamé gown which Mrs. Bartreau had chosen for her from the tinseled wardrobe in this room.

The Madam's gaze seemed to strip her naked. She knew the eyes of those men out there would do the same in another minute; it was something she had to endure.

"Magnifique!" Madam Bartreau trilled in her spurious Parisian accent. She had never been closer to France than the Vieux Carre in New Orleans. "You will set men's hearts aflame, *cherie.* By the comparison you make my other girls look like a kennel full of mongrel bitches."

Becky thought, shuddering, "By all means call a spade a spade," and turned back to the mirror on the pretext of giving her coiffure a final pat. Her hair was a rich shade of auburn, drawn back from her ears so as to give prominence to the false luster of the Madam's rhinestone clips which dangled from her earlobes. A flashy brooch of paste diamonds was pinned to her gown at the cleft of her bosom and a dozen of Madam Bartreau's bracelets, originally manufactured for the Indian squaw trade, jangled on her slim wrists.

"Marrying Dwayne would have almost been preferable to this," she thought miserably, and blinked back the tears as she followed Madam Bartreau's bulk through the heavy plush curtains which gave access from the dressing room to the narrow elevated stage overlooking the dance floor.

She remained in the shadow of the wings awaiting her cue as Madam Bartreau waddled out into the dazzling glare of the coal-oil footlights. The consumptive piano player who had been introduced to her earlier this evening as "The Perfessor" struck up a fanfare on his untuned melodeon, his music drowned out by the tumult of boot-stomping and hand-clapping from the cowboys and saloon riffraff who packed the floor out front.

Madam Bartreau's raucous whiskey voice came to her ears like something out of a bad dream:

"—Ladeez and gentlemen, it is now my great pleasure to produce the lovely mademoiselle for whom you have waited so patiently—the one, the only, Montana Meadowlark, the gorgeous and ravishing beauty herself, Mademoiselle Madeline—"

Becky Mullinary was scarcely conscious of the tumult of whistles and risqué shouts which greeted her demure entrance into the footlights' glare. Like an automaton she moved to stage center as the Madam retired to the dusky shadows of the wings.

Her face, cameo-perfect under the grotesque make-up the Madam insisted upon, was set into a frozen smile. Her eyes could not penetrate the blinding glare of the lights; the sea of faces out there was dim under milky layers of drifting tobacco smoke. She could feel the animal warmth of those unwashed bodies, blending with the raw smell of whiskey.

The clamor subsided as the girl nodded to the Perfessor, who struck the opening chords of *Londonderry Air.* From the moment she opened her lips to sing, a miracle of absolute silence went over the coarse-visaged throng. They had come to jeer, having from long experience with Madam Bartreau's flamboyant advertising learned to expect the worst.

Instead they heard a pure, flute-like soprano lifted in a simple Irish air which, as the banner outside the saloon had promised, put a lump in every throat and a tear in every eye.

It was the wholesome, virginal voice of a rarely gifted singer, completely alien to the brassy chanting these men had been accustomed to from honkytonk entertainers.

When she had finished, Becky Mullinary stood waiting for applause which never came. The dismaying thought went through her that she had failed to please her audience; it was not until afterwards that she realized that in their very silence the Paris Casino's patrons had given her a tribute far more sincere than any amount of cheering.

She had chosen *Those Endearing Young Charms* for her second number, and this time the applause came in a swelling, raucous roar which led to encore after encore.

The clock over the ornate bar pointed to ten o'clock when Madam Bartreau joined her on stage and, putting her flabby lips close to Becky's ear, said unctuously, "They're eatin' out of your hands, sweetie. But this is enough for one session. Those hoodlums don't buy likker when they're listenin' to your songs, and my girls won't earn anything if they don't dance."

Flushed and confident now in the glow of her unprecedented success, a success achieved without giving the men the usual ribald and smutty lyrics they were accustomed to from the Madam's entertainers, Becky Mullinary threw a kiss to the crowd and ran to the welcome sanctuary of the dressing room.

Madam Bartreau lumbered in after her, wheezing enthusiastically, "Keep this up and I'll boost your pay to sixty a week, Madeline honey. I'll lay odds that a month from now half the honkies in town will lock their doors for lack of business."

Becky declined the bottle of rye whiskey which the Madam produced from a drawer of the dressing table.

"I—I don't drink, thank you," she said. "Alcohol is injurious to the voice, you know—"

The Madam gulped from the neck of the bottle, wiped her mustached upper lip with the back of a flabby hand, and purred understandingly, "Sure, dearie. I fergot. You're class. You ain't one of these broken-down whores I'm used to hiring. You—"

A discreet knock sounded on the outer door. The Madam winked suggestively.

"Don't worry, dollie. I'll keep the sheepherders and the muleskinners from pestering you. I'll let 'em know you ain't available for the upstairs trade. Yessiree."

Becky shuddered, revulsion again overcoming the happy glow she had felt from the genuine tribute the audience had heaped upon her so lavishly. She thought, "Maybe I'll be able to stand it, after all—"

Seated at her dressing table, she had a view in the blemished glass of Madam Bartreau's elephantine posterior blocking the doorway. She was engaged in whispered conversation with a man out there, and Becky saw the Madam ease the door shut in the patron's face and turn to her, her bulbous cheeks flushed with excitement.

"It's the biggest man in the Territory, wanting to pay his compliments to you, dearie. Mr. Greg Costaine, who owns the big Butcherblock combine. The richest man in the Territory, they say. I told him you'd be glad to see him."

EIGHT

Becky felt a tremor of alarm sweep through her. Greg Costaine was a familiar name to her. She had heard vague rumors of the weight this cattle king carried in Territorial politics; she had heard her father predict that the beef-raising giant east of the Cascades might be Washington's first governor, when this country achieved full statehood.

She heard herself protesting, "I am very tired, Madam. Please convey my apologies to Mr. Costaine—"

Madam Bartreau's beady eyes narrowed to slits. She reached down to grab Becky's arm, the pressure of her beringed fingers cutting into the girl's flesh.

"Listen. You can't get high and mighty and snub a man like Greg Costaine, dearie." The Madam's voice carried a heavy undertone of menace. "I'm lucky to have a man of his kind even set foot inside of my place. You'll be nice to him, understand?"

Becky said limply, "But you promised—I wouldn't

have to mingle with your customers, like a percentage girl—you hired me to sing—"

Pure hate was in the Madam's contorted face as she whispered savagely, "Mr. Costaine is different. When he says 'frog,' people hop, you understand? No dance-hall singer can play snooty to a gentleman like Costaine. Now put on your best smile . . . *smile,* damn you!"

Releasing her grip on Becky's arm, Madam Bartreau lumbered to the door and vanished outside. Before the girl could get her panicked nerves under control the door opened and a tall, not unhandsome man stepped inside and closed the door, greeting her with a courtly bow.

"Miss Madeline, I am deeply honored. Your performance enchanted me. Allow me to introduce myself. I am Gregory Costaine—your humble servant and devoted admirer."

Becky Mullinary came to her feet, fighting the waves of weakness which made her legs tremble. Costaine was an imperious-looking man in his early fifties, his florid face set off with prematurely white hair. He wore a fustian clawhammer coat and polished Wellington boots under buckskin-foxed California pants. Diamonds glittered on his white shirt under a string cravat. She saw the brass buckle of a gun belt beneath his bed-of-flowers vest.

"Thank you—Mr. Costaine—"

Costaine stepped forward, snapped his spurred boots together like a cavalier and bent to brush her fingertips with his lips.

"Indeed? You've heard of me in Montana?" His voice carried a pompous artificiality which hinted that this rancher was a man of better than average education. "That is most flattering. However, I got my start in the cattle business over on the Musselshell, twenty years ago."

Towering over her, Greg Costaine dwarfed the slim girl. He was four inches over six feet tall. The sweet odor of whiskey on his breath told her that Costaine was slightly drunk.

"It amazes me to hear a voice like yours in a cheap dump like the Madam's," Costaine went on, hanging his coffee-brown Stetson over the back of a chair and seating himself beside the vanity table. "Please sit down, Miss Madeline. I should like to get better acquainted. I am very fortunate that a little business deal brought me to Coulee Center in time for your premiere performance. I hope I shall see a lot of you in weeks to come."

Becky sat down, against her own volition, because her knees suddenly refused to support her weight. The cattle king leaned forward, lamplight flashing on the gold nugget watch chain looped across his vest, and placed a big hand on her knee.

The touch of his fingers so familiarly placed sent a shudder through the girl. She slid her chair back out of his reach, and the withdrawal made Costaine pull his eyes away from her low-cut gown to stare at her with a bright and wicked interest.

"A hard-to-get gal, eh?" he laughed, reaching inside

his coat for a cigar. "You do not mind if I smoke? These perfectos were imported from Cuba. Women do not find them offensive."

She remained mute, conscious of a welling nausea within her. He bit off the tip of his cigar with teeth that had gold caps on them, spat the tobacco aside and thrust the weed between his lips. They were very white by contrast to his wax-tipped mustache.

"Uh—you live upstairs, I presume?"

The way he phrased the question brought a flush of color to the girl's marble-white cheeks.

"I—temporarily, yes. I plan to book accommodations over at the Elkhorn House tomorrow—"

Costaine tugged a fat turnip watch from his vest, snapped open the lid and said thickly, "Ten-fifteen. You have another performance at eleven, I understand?"

She nodded, not liking the hot desire in his eyes.

"Yes, Mr. Costaine. If you would excuse me now—I would like to rest before my next performance—"

Costaine nodded. "By all means. This room stinks of the Madam's eau de cologne." He thumbnailed a match into flame and held it to his cigar, his eyes regarding her lasciviously. "Suppose we go up to your room, Miss Madeline. I have some very choice bourbon with me. It would be good for your nerves."

She came to her feet then, cold with anger but no longer unsure of what she must do to cope with this man.

"You presume too much, Mr. Costaine. It is not in my contract to—to entertain the customers—upstairs.

47

I must ask you to leave now."

Greg Costaine stood up, putting his cigar on the dressing table and rubbing his palms together. Before Becky Mullinary was aware of his purpose the cattleman reached out both hands to seize her bare shoulders, pulling her to him with a savage urgency which caught her wholly unprepared.

His right hand slid down her shoulder blades, splayed fingers gliding under the hem of her gown, his left hand cupping her chin and tilting her face up toward his.

"Do I look like a tinhorn sport who'd soil himself on the Madam's percentage girls, Madeline?" he whispered, passion turning his pupils to pinpoints. "I am Greg Costaine. I am impatient with coyness, with false modesty."

"But—please—I have to rest up for my next—"

"I've already fixed it with the Madam so you won't have to be on stage at eleven."

His mouth came down, sealing her strangled outcry as she struggled impotently in his crushing embrace, tasting the tobacco and whiskey on his lips. She got her hands free and began to pound his chest with balled fists, her body arching back as he crowded harder against her, bending her over a chair back.

She felt herself going faint. She had no knowledge of the door opening. She was only conscious of Costaine suddenly releasing his grip on her and wheeling around to face the tall, grim-jawed man who was kicking the door shut with a spurred cowboot, a man dressed in the rough garb of an ordinary cowboy, but a man whose interruption came like an answer to prayer.

"Banning, what in hell do you mean breaking in here—"

The stranger's gunmetal eyes flicked across to Becky and his voice carried a cold menace as he answered Costaine's bull-like roar with the softest of tones: "The lady wasn't enjoying your advances, Greg. We'll both leave."

Becky fell back against the wall beside the dressing table, a hand to her mouth, her throat frozen as she saw Banning brace himself as Costaine whipped back his coat tails to grab the checked walnut stock of his low-slung Colt.

Before the cattleman could make his draw Banning moved in, teeth set in a half-snarl, his right fist coming up in a savage blow too rapid for her eye to follow.

The meaty, sodden impact of Banning's knuckles sledging the point of Costaine's jaw was like granite splintering under a maul. Becky saw Costaine's white leonine head snap back, a grunt escaping his throat. The power of Banning's uppercut was enough to drive the big man violently back against the mirror, to send slivered shards of glass raining down over the crystal bottle of cologne and pomade arrayed there.

Costaine was out on his feet. His huge frame buckled at hip and knee and as he fell his shoulders and elbows dragged the perfume bottle off the vanity.

Costaine came to rest in a seated position against the dressing table, propped up there like a corpse, blood welling from the bruise on his jaw. His head tilted for-ward over his chest so that the oozing red drops hit the nugget links of his watch chain and swelled glistening on the golden loops.

Becky Mullinary tore her gaze off the unconscious face of her attacker, lifted her eyes to meet Banning's. She saw the white heat of temper under the tan of his weathered skin, saw the tight stress of his lips gradually soften.

His clubbed fists unloosened and he reached up to doff his flat-crowned Stetson, a hint of a smile touching his mouth.

"I heard you sing, ma'am," Banning drawled. "I hope you won't mind me busting in like this—but when I heard scufflin'—"

"Oh—thank God you did," Becky whispered brokenly, overcome with the realization of her deliverance. "I can never tell you what it meant to me, Mr.— Mr.—"

"The name is Wes Banning, ma'am. I wanted to ask you—"

He broke off, suddenly embarrassed, and the girl said quickly, "Ask me what, Mr. Banning?"

"To ask you if you would marry me. Right away. Tonight."

NINE

Banning saw an expression that carried an admixture of disillusion and incredulity sweep the girl's face as her lips repeated his fantastic words.

"You—you're joking, of course," she said. "You

don't appear to be intoxicated—"

Banning twisted his hat in his hands, suddenly unsure of himself. He said, "I ain't joking and I'm cold sober, ma'am. I didn't mean it to sound so cold-blooded."

He glanced around the room and made a gesture that took in the racks of gaudy costumes, the faded theater bills tacked to the walls, all the tawdry accoutrements of a dance-hall dressing room. "You wouldn't have to leave all this—you wouldn't even see me again after tonight, ma'am."

To her own surprise, Becky Mullinary found herself suddenly sympathetic with this awkward, boyish man. Even with the unconscious Costaine sprawled between them, with the taste of him still curdling her tongue, she felt completely at ease and wholly unafraid of this ruggedly handsome stranger.

"This—this is the quaintest proposal a girl ever had," Becky said, laughter rushing in to fill the vacuum of her emotions. "You ask me to be your wife in one breath—and then say you never want to see me again. Should I be flattered?"

Wes Banning's face took on a scarlet hue.

"It ain't for the reason you may think," he groped desperately to express himself. "You see—it's like this. I own a two-bit cowspread back in the hills this side of the divide. Circle B. This hombre who was crowding his attentions on you is after my ranch—"

"Mr. Costaine," she cut in. "I understand he is a very powerful man."

Banning's mouth twisted bitterly.

"I hate Costaine as I never expect to hate any living man, Miss. He's aimin' to steal range I got under lease, and there's only one way I can stop him short of killing him. That's by filing claim to some land. And under the homestead law, I got to be married to somebody, in order to do it."

Becky said gently, the laughter going out of her eyes as she realized how deadly in earnest this man was, "Why did you select me, of all the girls in Coulee Center, Mr. Banning? If any female of marriageable age will do, I should think there would have been others more accessible to such a strange plan—"

Banning's big hands fumbled with his Stetson brim.

"I—I couldn't stomach any of the Madam's dance-hall jezebels, ma'am," he said. "Besides which I couldn't depend on any of them not to double-cross me if Costaine got to 'em. But, you, seeing you on the stage—I got the idea you'd be—well, reliable—"

He broke off, suddenly grinning. "I guess I been a fool, lady. I had it figgered that you probably wouldn't be working in Coulee City permanently, and it is my understanding that a wife who ain't even been kissed could get any judge in the land to annul the marriage—"

He thought of something then and turned his back on the girl to latch the door against Madam Bartreau's possible return. Then, crossing the room, he stooped to lift Greg Costaine's dead weight and, as easily as if he were carrying a sack of grain, carried the unconscious man over to the alley window.

Bracing Costaine's sagging bulk across one knee while he got the window open, without further ceremony the Circle B rider dumped Costaine's inert shape into the dust of the black alley outside. He was grinning to himself when he faced Becky again.

"He'd have been ugly when he come to," Banning explained. "You see, Costaine come to town today to file on that land next to my ranch. That's why I wanted to locate a girl who'd marry me tonight, so I could beat him to the land office. I guess I was plumb crazy to even entertain such an idea. You got ample reason to be offended, ma'am. I'm sorry."

Becky Mullinary twisted a lace handkerchief in her fingers.

"Don't apologize, Mr. Banning," she whispered. "It was just a business proposition. You—are a very kind person, Mr. Banning. I want you to know how much I respect you, how grateful I am for what you did for me tonight. But—I couldn't—let myself—marry a stranger—even when it would mean absolutely nothing."

Banning still stood beside the open window, the cool night wind ruffling the black hair at his temples. He straddled the window sill now, adjusting the lanyard of his Stetson under the firm angle of his jaw.

"Thanks for puttin' it that way," he said. "The Madam didn't see me come in. Reckon I'll duck out the window. No hard feelin's, ma'am?"

Becky shook her head, fighting a constriction in her throat.

"Of course not. You—you'll find somebody else—to

53

help you out, Mr. Banning?"

He shrugged. "Reckon not. It wouldn't have worked out, I can see that. I hope this mess won't get you in dutch with the Madam. She's a witch, that Madam is . . . So long."

He was gone then, leaving only the open window for her to stare at. It seemed that this whole mad episode had been a figment of her overwrought imagination, that Costaine and Banning had never existed. Only the shattered silver fragments of the mirror littering the floor, the spilled bottles and the drop of blood on the carpet remained to attest the reality of what had happened.

Reality, the consequences she must face when the Madam returned to this room, flooded through the girl now, making her as physically afraid as she had been struggling in Costaine's arms.

She suddenly knew that she could never step out on the Casino's stage again, no matter how desperately she needed the money Madam Bartreau would pay her. Coulee Center had promised a refuge from a fate that had put her to flight; now it seemed that she was caught in a maelstrom from which there would be no escape short of suicide.

Wes Banning had offered her an avenue of escape. Marriage that would not be a real marriage in any sense of the word . . . a mere bit of legal chicanery to forestall the evil designs of Greg Costaine.

With a little cry, Becky Mullinary opened the rear door of the dressing room and fled up the dark stairs to the dreaded "upstairs" portion of the Casino. She entered the tiny cubicle she shared with Straight-Edge Sal, half afraid she might find the bed occupied, and without daring to light the lamp she ripped off the decollete gown of silver lamé and kicked off the French heeled silver slippers.

When she had divested herself of the Madam's gaudy jewelry she drew her leather portmanteau out from under her cot, the only luggage she had carried with her in her flight from Seattle three weeks ago. With frenzied haste she packed her few belongings and put on the simple gray suit and aigrette-feathered hat she had been wearing when she had alighted from the Ellensburg stage this morning.

Her room, like all the other cribs on this floor, opened on a railed balcony overlooking a weedy back yard. There was an outside fire-escape ladder leading from the balcony and she descended it, bag in hand, reasonably certain no one had witnessed her furtive departure from the Casino building.

She entered the black gut of the alley leading to the main street, avoiding the sprawled shape of Greg Costaine huddled under the window of her dressing room.

She could hear the cattleman's stertorous breathing as she passed the bar of lamplight, relieved to note that the Madam had not yet returned to the dressing room.

Reaching the street, Becky flung a wild glance in both directions, having no way of knowing where Wes Banning might have gone.

The fates that ruled her unhappy destiny smiled on

Becky Mullinary then, for she caught sight of the Circle B rancher's tall, angular shape crossing the wheel-rutted street in the direction of the livery barn diagonally opposite the Casino.

Her choked call arrested Banning at the far side of the street. He halted, staring at her with jaw unhinged in surprise as she stumbled through the ankle deep dust to his side.

"Mr. Banning—please—"

His strong hand caught her as she swayed, fighting off a tide of faintness.

"The Madam fired you, ma'am? I was afraid of that—she's got to kow-tow to Costaine—he's her land-lord—"

She peered up at him, tears wetting her cheeks now.

"Mr. Banning, I'm ready to marry you tonight—pro-viding you'll grant me one favor in return?"

"A favor, ma'am?"

"Yes. I must get away from this awful town. I'll marry you—under the terms you gave me—providing you'll take me with you to your ranch."

TEN

A scowl put a notch between Banning's brows.

"Take you—with me? That wasn't part of my plan, ma'am. I wouldn't hold you to a thing, you got my pledge word on that. You see, Circle B is a pretty wild and lonely place. Not fit for a girl—"

Becky Mullinary shuddered to the wild hammering

on her pulses, letting him take her portmanteau and following him over to the blank wall of the livery stable where they would be out of the glare of the Paris Casino's oil torches.

"You said—we wouldn't really be married to each other—just in name only, so you could get this land you need to fight Mr. Costaine. Am I asking too much—to want to go with you, Mr. Banning? You see—"

"You can talk to me, ma'am. If you're in some kind of trouble—"

She said heavily, "You know nothing about me, Mr. Banning. The risk is as much yours as mine. You don't even know my real name. You see—I'm running away from something. For all you know, I may be a criminal of some kind—"

Wes Banning said gently, "If it's a hideout you're looking for, ma'am, I reckon Circle B is made to order for you. It's ninety miles up in the hills. Fifteen from the nearest town, Medicine Lodge. Nobody ever visits the ranch. And you won't have to tell me anything about your past, nothing at all. You'll be free to pull stakes any time you take a notion to."

She drew herself together, trying to shut her ears to the Casino porch, announcing the Montana Meadowlark's second appearance of the evening.

"Call me—Rebecca—or Becky," she said. "Madeline is just my—my stage name."

"Becky," Wes Banning whispered, rolling the name over his tongue, savoring the ring of it. "I like that name, Becky. Mine's Wes."

He tugged a watch from his levis pocket.

"Crowdin' eleven," he said. "Probably have to roust the Baptist parson out of his bunk. His missus can be the witness."

Twenty minutes later, in the austerely furnished parlor of the Baptist parsonage on a side street, Wesley Banning and Rebecca Mullinary stood before the puckish-faced little Coulee Center man of God and repeated their vows.

"You—uh—have a ring, Wes?" the preacher asked, pausing in the ceremony and clearing his throat.

Banning hesitated, then reached inside his hickory shirt and drew out a plain gold band which he wore around his neck in a loop of rawhide. He untied the thong and handed the ring to Rev. Prothero.

"It was my mother's," he whispered to the girl at his side. "Her legacy to me when she died bringin' me into the world."

Moments later, Wes Banning heard a voice that seemed oddly apart from himself repeating Rev. Prothero's solemn words, "With this ring, I thee wed. For richer, for poorer, in sickness and in health . . . till death do us part . . ."

Then it was over, and the parson's matronly wife, bundled in a corduroy robe to hide her night clothes, her gray hair in curl papers, was tittering self-consciously, "Well, young man, aren't you going to kiss your bride?"

Banning turned to the girl at his side, sensing the empty travesty he was making of what by heritage of custom should be one of life's holiest moments.

• • •

In the soft wash of lamplight the girl's face was ethereally beautiful. Before the ceremony Becky had retired to a place of privacy with Mrs. Prothero and had washed off the heavy theatrical makeup she had been wearing. The parson's wife had fixed a pink rosebud in the lapel of her suit and Banning's eyes rested on that tiny flower now, his mind straying to all the talks he had had with Donna Fleming about the bridal bouquet he would some day buy her. "White roses and forget-me-nots and baby-breath fern, Wes, just like a society wedding in the city—"

He felt Becky's slim hands trembling as they sought his, and unwillingly he faced a mental picture of Donna's hands resting on the shoulders of the cheap gambler in her room at the Elkhorn House tonight. Where was Donna now? In DeWitt's arms—or laughing with him at a table in the Casino, waiting for the Montana Meadowlark to make her second appearance on the Madam's stage?

Donna's envisioned face faded from Banning's thoughts as he bent his head and pressed his lips briefly against this girl's, this girl whom he had never laid eyes upon until two hours ago, this girl who was now his lawfully wedded wife, whom he had promised, perjuring his heart, to honor and cherish forever . . .

They left the parsonage after Rev. Prothero had affixed his signature to the marriage certificate. The courthouse clock was chiming eleven forty-five when they arrived at the door of Paul Priggee's lean-to home.

59

The venerable old land agent opened the door to their knock and, not having his spectacles, could not clearly see the face of the young woman Banning escorted into the redolent warmth of the room.

"You had me worried, Donna," Priggee said genially. "The way time was running on, I thought maybe you'd shied off and left your man to face Costaine alone."

Becky's eyes held their unspoken hurt as she shook hands with the oldster. With the full lamplight striking her face, Priggee saw his mistake and confusion stormed across his face in a red tide.

"My wife, Rebecca Banning," the Circle B man said roughly. "Becky, this is Mr. Priggee, I told you about."

Priggee choked out an embarrassed acknowledgment and hurried to bring up his Morris chair for the girl.

"If you'll excuse a blundering old fool for a few minutes, ma'am," he said awkwardly, "Wes and I will make out the homestead papers in my front office."

Becky nodded, her hands twisting the hem of her suit coat as she stared down at her lap.

"Surely, Mr. Priggee. I understand."

Out in the front office, Priggee got a lamp lighted after he had secured the window shades facing the street. The agent's face held a confused questioning as he opened his safe and drew out a dossier of legal forms.

"I—uh—had the papers made out in full," he apologized sheepishly, "but with Donna Fleming's name in them. I hope you'll forgive a half-blind old galoot for—"

"Donna turned me down cold, Paul. Seems she aims

to marry that roulette croupier over at the White Palace."

Priggee busied himself at his desk, his pen scratching noisily in the silence as he filled in the application blank which would make the south section at the mouth of Chinook Gap the legal property of Mrs. Rebecca M. Banning.

As he copied the girl's name off the marriage certificate, Priggee shot a glance under his cowled eyebrows at the stony-faced cowpuncher opposite his desk. Banning said dully,

"She's that singer from the Paris Casino, Paul. That's all I can tell you about her."

Priggee dipped his pen in the ink bottle and extended it for Banning to sign the papers as Becky's lawfully wedded husband.

"You'll pardon me for saying it, Wes, but she doesn't have the look of a honkytonk woman. I think you drew a thoroughbred out of the pack."

Banning shrugged. "Whatever she is, I won't be laying a hand on her, Paul. This is a strictly business deal. Becky is going into it with her eyes open."

They carried the papers out to the back room and the girl signed under Banning's name in her delicate Spencerian. Her eyes were moist as she read her marriage name for the first time: *Rebecca Mullinary Banning . . .*

"This is your copy," Priggee said, handing a paper to Banning. "The two of you now control the entrance to Chinook Gap. That's the news I'll have for Costaine when he shows up with Lattimer in the morning. I'll tell 'em all this was transacted before five o'clock. God bless you both."

Banning extended a hand to the land official, knowing the acute risk this man had run on their behalf tonight. Priggee could face a penitentiary sentence for falsification of public records, violating his oath of office, if he were discovered.

"We won't forget this favor, Paul," Banning said huskily.

Priggee pressed thumb and finger against his eyes, feeling suddenly old and tired.

"If it'll help scuttle Costaine," he said, "the risks will be worth the cost. Mrs. Banning, I wish you much happiness. Wes is a fine man. I once advised him not to settle in Butcherblock's path. The fact that he did shows you his worth."

The twelve strokes of midnight were reverberating between the Coulee cliffs when Banning and the girl walked out on the main street, listening to the din inside Madam Bartreau's. Both wondered if Greg Costaine was still sprawled out in the alley. By now the Madam surely knew her star attraction had vanished . . .

"It's a long ride to the ranch," Wes Banning said. "I'll rent a buckboard—"

"No—I prefer horseback," she said. "Just so—we get out of this terrible place as quickly as possible."

He saw the pleading in her eyes, and wondered what lay behind her fear, what ghost of the past might be pursuing her. A rush of tenderness poured through him as he realized how literally they stood on the threshold of a new life together, temporary and spurious though their union of mutual convenience was foredoomed to be.

At the door of Cy Crowfant's barn, Becky asked softly, "Wes,"—it was the first time his first name had left her lips—"will you forgive—one tiny bit of feminine curiosity, if I promise never to mention it again?"

He set her portmanteau down and nodded, waiting.

"Who is—Donna?"

His glance ran unthinkingly along the street toward the lighted window of Room 7 at Elkhorn House.

"Donna?" he said meagerly. "Why, Donna is a woman who wanted a better honeymoon than I'm offering you, Becky."

He left her to enter the barn to rent horses for their wedding journey. Becky gazed up at the unearthly glitter of the stars, so infinitely more vivid than she had ever seen them in the Puget Sound country, and whispered to the night, "Whoever you are, Donna, I think you made a very great mistake."

ELEVEN

Dawn's first slant of ruddy light struck the window of Greg Costaine's room on the second floor of the Elkhorn House and roused the Butcherblock boss from a troubled sleep.

He swung his booted legs off the bed and sat up, his brain swelling as if to burst the confines of his skull, and tried to figure out how he had got here. When he moved his jaw it felt like a broken hinge and as he lifted trembling fingers to touch the fresh scab on his chin the pain of it snapped him back to reality. "That damn' Banning," he rumbled thickly, coming to his feet and clinging to the bedpost until the room stopped spinning around him.

Lattimer, his foreman, with the help of one of Madam Bartreau's house bouncers, had carried him up here and stretched him on his bed, fully clad. He had only the haziest recollection of Lattimer's finding him in the dust of the alley outside the Paris Casino. The thick alkali powder still clung to his swallowtail coat, smudged the rumpled counterpane on the bed.

He remembered telling Lattimer to "Get Banning for me if it takes you all night." Presumably his ramrod hadn't carried out his orders, for the other bed next to his had not been slept in, and now it was daylight.

Costaine stumbled over to the marble-topped washstand, emptied a pitcher of water into a big china bowl, and soused his head thoroughly, scooping water up with both hands. He toweled himself and was searching his pockets for a comb when he found the pint flask of bourbon he had planned to split with the pretty singer over at the Casino. The recollection of his brief struggle with "Mademoiselle Madeline" filled him with a sharp anger that served to clear the cobwebs in his head.

It was hard to say which had galled him deepest, the girl's resistance to his lovemaking or his knockout at the hands of his former cowhand, Wes Banning.

Costaine was taking a swig from the whiskey bottle when the door opened and his foreman, Chet Lattimer, shuffled into the room. Lattimer had been a brush-popper from the brasada flats of the Nueces country in west Texas when Costaine had hired him for a trail drive to Montana. He was a big, rawboned man whose prominent cheekbones and thick black hair and black eyes attested to a strain of Comanche blood in his veins.

At the moment Lattimer looked dead beat, his eyes red-rimmed from booze and a sleepless night, stubble thick on his blunt jaw, his face harrowed deep with fatigue.

"Turned this burg inside out, boss, and didn't locate Banning for you," Lattimer said. "Just found out from Cy Crowfant that he pulled out of Coulee around midnight, just about the time the Madam located you out in that alley."

Costaine flushed, thanking his lucky stars that no one else had discovered him, or his humiliation would be common gossip throughout the county by now.

"All the better," Costaine growled. "I'll ride out to the Gap and square accounts with that bastard myself. I ain't been manhandled like that since I was a kid in San Antone, Chet."

Lattimer dragged Durham sack and papers from his rusty vest and began building a smoke.

"Boss," the Butcherblock ramrod said uncertainly, "the Madam tells me that singer gal is still missin' this morning. Vamosed. Took her things with her. The

Madam ain't seen her since she let you go into her dressin' room."

Costaine started dragging a comb through his snarled roach of silver hair.

"Don't mention that little witch again, you savvy, Chet?"

Lattimer fired his cigarette. "There's something you ought to know," he said. "Crowfant says Banning rented two horses. A woman left town with him. I got a hunch it might have been that honkytonk singer."

Costaine froze, turning this information over in his head. During the years Banning had been on his payroll, Costaine had come to know beyond any doubt that the man was not a woman-chaser like the typical cowpuncher. Furthermore, he was engaged to marry the pretty young seamstress, Donna Fleming.

"No," Costaine said finally. "If Banning lit a shuck with a woman, that woman was Donna Fleming, not a dance-hall floozy."

"Crowfant said it wasn't Donna, boss."

Costaine's eyes narrowed. A dismaying possibility was worming into his head.

"Chet," he said, reaching for the expensive Stetson which Lattimer had hung on the bedpost for him last night, "we better get over to Priggee's land office. I got a hunch Banning might have come to town after he found where Karnhizel cut his fence yesterday morning and tried to rig a deal to get title to that south section before you filed on it."

Buttoning his fustian coat over the telltale bloodstains on his vest, Greg Costaine left the hotel with Lattimer at his side, the big foreman having to stretch his legs to keep up with the cattle baron's reaching stride.

They found the government land agent, Paul Priggee, out pumping a bucket of water in the back yard behind his living quarters. Priggee said nothing by way of greeting when he found Costaine and Lattimer waiting at his door.

"Priggee, we got some business to transact with you this morning," Costaine snapped sourly. "Lattimer here wants to file a homestead claim."

The old man thumbed his suspenders over his skinny shoulders and shook his head adamantly.

"It's barely six o'clock," he reminded them surlily. "I open the office for business at eight, not a minute before."

Costaine moved to block the oldster's doorway.

"Hold on. Lattimer's got his eye on Section 33 at the east entrance of Chinook Gap. You carry this county in your head. You can tell us if it's open for entry."

Priggee narrowed his eyes. "Section 33?" he repeated. "You're too late by one day. Section 33 has been taken up."

Lattimer broke the following silence. "Who by?"

The land agent tongued his cheek, gauging the dangerous tempers of this pair.

"Wesley Banning and his wife. Now stand aside, Costaine, and let me by. I got breakfast to cook."

Costaine's bleary eyes showed the shock of Priggee's news. He seemed incapable of movement as Priggee shoved past him into the lean-to. But when the agent went to close the door, Costaine thrust a beefy shoulder against it. His eyes burned with pure menace as he snarled, "Banning married? Since when?"

Priggee shrugged. "Since yesterday, I reckon. Least-wise his marriage papers were in order, making his Missus eligible to take over Section 33 under the law."

Chet Lattimer, standing at the foot of the steps, asked sharply: "Who'd he marry? It couldn't have been Donna Fleming. I seen her goin' into the Casino with Cecil DeWitt an hour after Banning left town—"

Priggee's answer was to shove his door shut in Costaine's face and bolt it from the inside. Costaine turned as he felt Lattimer's hand on his arm.

"Boss, there's somethin' damn' fishy about this. Crowfant told me Banning didn't get to town until yesterday sundown. Even if he got hisself married the minute he hit town, he didn't have time to file on that section before Priggee's office closed. I say that Priggee's lyin'."

TWELVE

A slow grin broke through the anger on Costaine's face.

"Chet," he said, "you got something there. If Priggee ain't lyin', then he pulled a sandy on us. Come on, I got an idea. If it fits, we'll have Paul Priggee over a barrel."

Lattimer followed his boss up the alley to the side

street and saw Costaine turn left, in the opposite direction from the center of town.

"Where we goin', boss?"

"To Parson Prothero's. The justice of the peace is up in Medicine Lodge this week. Prothero's the only man this side of Wenatchee who could have performed a weddin' ceremony for Banning."

Arriving at the Baptist parsonage, they were delayed a considerable interval before the parson's pudgy wife appeared at the door, blinking sleepily.

"Did the reverend perform a weddin' ceremony yesterday, Missus Prothero?" Costaine demanded without preliminaries.

The matron nodded, awed by her first face-to-face meeting with Foothill County's most fabulous citizen. Butcherblock, alone out of all the roundabout cattle outfits, had never contributed anything to the upkeep of the Coulee Center church.

"Why, yes—yes he did, Mr. Costaine," the minister's wife admitted. "It was that nice Mr. Banning who used to work for—"

"When did this happen, Missus Prothero?"

The woman hesitated, detecting the note of menace in the cattleman's voice. "We-el, I guess it's public information, sir. Ezra and I had gone to bed. It was after eleven." She tittered. "It was so romantic, Mr. Costaine. An elopement, I reckon 'twas."

Costaine sucked in a long breath, measuring his words carefully. "Who did Banning marry?"

For the first time, doubt showed in Mrs. Prothero's eyes.

"I—I really couldn't say, sir. I never seen her around Coulee before. I know Ezra and me were surprised it wasn't that dressmaker. We always figgered young Wes would marry the Fleming girl, but it wasn't her."

Reverend Prothero, still in his flannel nightgown, padded up to the door behind his wife at this moment and stood squinting out at the two gun-hung cattlemen at his door.

"Anything wrong, Marthy?" he asked timorously.

"Plenty," barked Costaine. "Reverend, I want to look at your marryin' book. I'm right curious to know who Banning dabbed his loop on to, and when."

Ezra Prothero, a gentle man incapable of guile or suspicion of his fellow man's motives, invited the two cowmen into his sparsely-furnished parlor. His wife shuffled out of the room while Costaine and Lattimer stood by, waiting for Prothero to unlock a Victorian secretary desk and draw out his dog-eared book of matrimonial records.

"Here we are, gentlemen," Prothero beamed, opening the book for Costaine. "A charming girl she was, sweet and innocent-looking. As pretty as Donna Fleming, I'd say. She—"

Costaine grabbed the book from the minister and studied the latest entry.

"Rebecca Mullinary," he muttered. "Born in Spokane . . . United in holy wedlock at 11:25 p.m. . . ."

Without thanking the preacher for his trouble, Costaine turned on his heel and strode out of the parsonage, followed by Lattimer. When they reached the gate in the

70

picket fence, Costaine was laughing.

"What's so all-fired comical, boss?" Lattimer demanded testily. "Way I see this, Banning's out-foxed us, slapping his brand on that south section. That means if we try to run the herd into the Gap we'll have to cross his wife's homestead—"

Costaine only laughed the louder.

"It's no joshin' matter," Lattimer continued, his anger rising. "You may have the sheriff under yore thumb, boss, and the county commissioners. But shovin' our beef acrost a gover'ment homestead is somethin' else again. Don't you savvy how Banning's whipsawed us? He could call in a U.S. Marshal and slap a lien on ever' Butcherblock cow we put on his lease—"

"So he could, Chet, if his claim to Section 33 was legal."

"Priggee says he's recorded it already. That makes it legal for my money. You're the bull of the herd hereabouts, Greg, but damned if you're big enough to buck Uncle Sam."

They were heading up Main Street toward the hotel now, Costaine moving at a more leisurely pace.

"Think it over, Chet," Costaine said. "Banning got himself married to this Rebecca Mullinary, whoever she might be, around 11:30 last night. Priggee's land office locked up at five. Which means that either Banning wasn't married when his woman filed on that section—or else Priggee doctored the papers to read prior to five o'clock yesterday afternoon. At which time we can prove by Cy Crowfant that Banning

71

wasn't even in town."

Arriving at the Elkhorn's dining room, where a few early-rising commercial men were at breakfast, Lattimer said in a puzzled voice, "You mean we can shove our stock into the Gap, then? You figger Banning's wife ain't the legal owner of that south section?"

Costaine did not answer until they reached their customary table at the far corner of the dining hall.

"By the time we finish eating," he told his foreman, "Priggee will have his office open. I want you to sashay over there and demand to see Banning's application. Find out exactly when this Mullinary woman filed her claim. No matter when it was, we've got enough on Priggee to hang him."

As the two men from Butcherblock were finishing breakfast, the weekly Yakima-Okanogan stage rolled in and unloaded its mail and passengers in front of the hotel. Shortly thereafter a freckle-faced kid entered the hotel dining room to hawk the latest Seattle and Portland newspapers.

"On your way back from Priggee's office, stop by the stable and have Crowfant saddle our horses," Costaine ordered his segundo. "We'll head back home as soon as you get back."

After Lattimer had left on his errand Costaine whistled the newspaper boy over to his table and bought copies of the Portland *Oregonian* and the Seattle *Post-Intelligencer.* He turned at once to the latest beef market quotations.

That done, Costaine leafed idly through the other

pages of the Seattle paper, scanning the headlines and searching for news carrying the dateline of the Territorial capital, Olympia, in particular. As a potential candidate for the legislature at next year's election, Costaine had to keep himself abreast of Washington's political activities.

A headline on an inside page caught his attention briefly:

NO TRACE OF SOCIALITE
MISSING SINCE APRIL 3
Foul Play Feared as Step-Daughter
of Prominent Seattle Attorney
Vanishes on Eve of Wedding
to Wealthy Shipping Heir

Costaine would have ignored the following news story had it not been for the pen-and-ink portrait of a beautiful young woman which accompanied the piece.

There was no mistaking that likeness. The missing Seattle socialite was the singer whom Madam Bartreau had billed as Mademoiselle Madeline, the Montana Meadowlark. The caption under the picture read, "Miss Rebecca ('Becky') Mullinary, Vanished Fiancée of Dwayne Halverson, Scion of Black Funnel Steamship Lines Fortune."

His heart hammering his ribs, Greg Costaine scanned the newspaper account which followed:

Three weeks have elapsed since the mysterious disappearance of Rebecca Mullinary, 21-year-old step-daughter of Lester Hadley, prominent Seattle attorney, with no trace of her whereabouts having come to light at this writing.

Miss Mullinary was last seen at her home on Queen Anne Hill, preparing for her wedding to Mr. Dwayne Halverson, of the socially prominent shipping family of this city. Queried by reporters at his office, the girl's step-father denied any rift between Miss Mullinary and her millionaire fiancé.

"We feel she was kidnapped by Skidrow hoodlums," the distracted lawyer informed police, "although to this moment neither myself nor the Halverson family have received any ransom demands from her abductors."

Miss Mullinary achieved local distinction while an undergraduate at the University of Washington for her rare talents as a coloratura soprano. Police authorities in New York have been advised to keep a watch-out for the missing girl, on the chance that if she left of her own volition she might have gone east to visit relatives of her deceased father . . .

Clipping out the news item with his pocket knife, Greg Costaine was leaving the Elkhorn House when he met his foreman at the lobby door. Lattimer was grinning broadly.

"It was like you said, all right," the foreman reported. "Priggee run a sandy on us. He recorded the homestead application as of 4:40 yesterday afternoon—before Banning was married or before he was even in Coulee."

Costaine grinned mysteriously.

"Bring the horses over to the Overland Telegraph office," the Butcherblock boss ordered. "I've got a message to get off to Seattle. I have a hunch Banning's honeymoon won't last very long."

THIRTEEN

Despite the urgency he felt to return to Circle B as quickly as possible, Banning allotted two full days to the trek out of deference to Becky's comfort.

At noon following their departure from the county seat, Becky riding sidesaddle on one of Crowfant's rented mounts, they arrived at Anvil Ferry where Mrs. Linklater, the ferryman's wife, had prepared them a bountiful meal and turned her own bedroom over to Becky for an afternoon nap.

Forty miles of riding, coupled with the strain she had undergone at the Paris Casino, had reduced the girl to an utter exhaustion which no amount of willpower could mask from Wes Banning.

When the girl had to be roused for supper, Banning gave up any notion of riding on to Showalter's ranch that night. He had been careful to sidestep Mrs. Linklater's prying questions, giving her the idea that Rebecca Mullinary had relatives in Medicine Lodge and that rather than wait a week for the stage, she had elected to accept his escort for the journey.

That explanation satisfied Mrs. Linklater's rummaging curiosity, and explained Banning's reason for spreading his blankets that night in the haymow of Linklater's barn.

The next morning, Becky was riding astride on a stock saddle Banning had borrowed, along with a fresh horse, from Linklater. She had swapped her skirt for a pair of the ferryman's corduroy pants.

At Showalter's Lazy S ranch, Banning picked up his own horse, left there two days before. He found his friend's ranch deserted, Showalter's crew being out on the north range branding his winter's increase.

Between Lazy S and Circle B, they had to cover twenty-odd miles of Butcherblock range. In the distance Banning saw frequent evidence of the big round-up Lattimer's crew was engaged in. The fact that Costaine was consolidating his beef gather in a big pool herd on the Beaver Creek bottoms pointed up the cattle king's intention of hazing his herd to Chinook Gap as soon as his vast round-up operations were finished.

Grass was pitifully scant here on the broad leagues of Costaine's range. Winter erosion had stripped thousands of acres bare of any vegetation except the hardiest sagebrush, as a result of Butcherblock's over-grazing policy during the past decade. In the sterility of this once-fertile grassland Banning saw the reason why Costaine was forced to turn covetous eyes toward the thick greenery of Chinook Gap's fifty thousand acres of unspoiled range.

This second afternoon out of Coulee Center, Banning veered steadily northwestward, avoiding the cowtown at Medicine Lodge. As they drew near the outer limits of Butcherblock's territory, Banning had the proof of his own eyes that Costaine's round-up was nearly complete. A matter of days would see Butcherblock's twelve thousand head of hungry cattle moving toward the Gap.

They came in sight of Circle B land just as the sun was easing into its appointed notch of the snow-crusted Cascade range, spilling its golden light down the cliff-walled length of Chinook Gap.

They had spoken but seldom on this ninety-mile trek from the county seat, each occupied with personal problems not to be shared with the other. For Banning's part, he felt a relief at having traversed Butcherblock's range without having been met by bushwhackers put on his trail after his showdown with Costaine in Coulee Center.

Banning knew he could expect Costaine to strike back, and soon. Things were shaping up toward a bloody showdown or a total surrender on Butcherblock's part. The gravity of what lay ahead in the next few days was enough to crowd out of his thoughts any contemplation of his strange alliance with this beautiful, mysterious girl who rode at his stirrup.

Becky, for her part, seemed to be submerged in her own deep personal tragedy, whatever it was. She had offered no explanation for her reason for wanting to quit Coulee Center the very day she had arrived there to take a job at Madam Bartreau's brothel, and Banning had no intention of plying her with questions about her secret.

Thus they had made this long horseback trip in virtual silence, indrawn and aloof from each other. It was not until they topped the last hogback and caught sight of the Circle B corrals, barns and sod-roofed ranch house silhouetted against the glory of the day's end that Banning hipped around in saddle to regard this stranger to whom he was forty-eight hours married.

He saw her staring at the splendor of the landscape, her lovely face transformed into a shining testimonial of how deeply the grandeur of this wild and lonely scene enthralled her senses.

"Well, there's Circle B, Becky," he said reining up. "I warned you it was a sorry-looking uncurried neck of nowhere to bring a woman. I won't blame you for wanting to leave it."

Her firm young breasts stirred to a deep intake of breath. The ravages of fatigue from the gruelling hours in saddle under the punishing heat of a brassy April sky seemed to drop from Becky now like an unwanted garment as she regarded the silver flashings of Beaver Creek meandering out of the Gap, the cliffs making their protective wedge through the conifers of the further mountain slopes which lifted, terrace on terrace, to meet the granite teeth of the Cascade divide, with Mount Rainer's spectacular truncated stump dominating the southwestern skyline, the sunset colors turning it an ephemeral pink.

"It's—it's as close to heaven as I could ever hope to be, Wes," she said humbly.

He stared at her, knowing she was seeing this

untamed, raw outland at its scenic best, beautiful beyond all description as the twilight haze began pouring down the east slope in the wake of the sun's setting. He commented noncommittally,

"Well, it's lonely out here. But it can be rough. Snow three feet on the level for three months at a stretch. Wait till you see your first winter blizzard—"

His reference to the future brought the girl swinging around to study him, and he regretted the inadvertent inference that she might remain on Circle B that long. Under the circumstances it was unthinkable for either of them.

She caught something in his tightening cheeks which reminded her of her false status as his wife. She was an instrument of necessity, party to a sacred contract which would enable this tall and fined-down man to gain title to land which in turn would give him a bulwark against the overpowering might of Costaine's cattle syndicate.

Touched by a regret she herself could not immediately define or understand, Becky said hesitantly, "As long as you let me stay I will try to earn my keep, Wes. I can cook and sew and—keep house for you." She met his narrowing glance with frank candor. "Our contract works both ways, you know. You're free to tell me to leave—whenever the notion strikes you."

He jerked on the reins with unnecessary roughness and said, "Let's get along. All the crew I've got is a Yakima Injun buck. I hope he'll have a snack of bait ready for us."

Big Yak was returning from the barn with a pail of

warm milk when Banning and his bride dismounted in front of the log shack. The Indian's swarthy countenance remained woodenly inscrutable as he saw his boss give the girl a hand down from stirrups and untie her portmanteau from behind his cantle.

"Yak, this is my squaw," Banning said, adding something in the Indian's tongue of which the girl caught but two syllables she could understand: "Donna."

She thought, an unaccountable pain touching her, "Even this ignorant savage was expecting him to bring another woman back with him."

FOURTEEN

Big Yak ignored his introduction to Becky, pointing to a fresh cougar pelt which he had pegged down on the slab door of the cabin. It was a huge specimen, reaching from the ground to the rafters.

"Got um with Injun snare," Big Yak reported. "Ketchum when he come down to river to drink two sleeps ago. Finish um with ax. Now cubs starve, not eat cattle next spring. Good."

Banning congratulated his Indian cowhand on trapping the big cat, reflecting bleakly that only three days ago, ending the varmint's slaughter of his calves was the most serious problem he had to face. Now, with the imminent threat of Butcherblock's arrival at the Gap's drift fence, the cougar's importance paled to insignificance.

Banning took hold of the pleated rawhide latch string

and opened the door. He turned to Becky, and mistook her hesitation for revulsion at having to enter such a primitive home. He could not know the thought which crossed his bride's mind: "Will he be sentimental enough to carry me over the threshold the way a bride-groom is supposed to do?"

But Wes Banning merely took her arm and led her into the one-room shack. He was thinking, Donna wouldn't even come out to look my place over. Why should this poor kid find it any more desirable?

He saw Becky's eyes go moist as he stepped inside, glancing around the room, neatly kept as far as bach-elor quarters went, but totally and primitively mascu-line in its austerity.

Double bunks of split cedar poles were in a far corner. A pile of odoriferous beaver plews was piled on boards which formed a partial attic floor under the rafters. Bridles and saddles, oilskin slickers and odds and ends of man's clothing hung from wall pegs. A Winchester rifle was cradled in a spread of elk horns over the lavarock fireplace.

"Pretty terrible, eh?" Wes Banning said with wry humor. "Wouldn't blame you if you want to pull stakes tomorrow, ma'am—Becky. It's no fit place for a girl. I'd blush to bring a Siwash squaw here."

Becky said with simple sincerity, "It's cozy and—secure, Wes. I like it."

She helped Big Yak clear off the playing cards and other debris from the crude deal table in the center of the room, while Banning stoked the rusty cookstove with pine knots and checked the contents of an iron stew kettle where Big Yak had some tribal meat dish cooking.

Later, eating by the light of the open hearth, Becky thought she had never tasted anything more delectable than the dutch oven bread Banning had rustled up, rich with butter from Big Yak's churn, with wild clover honey taken from a bee tree above the North Rim to flavor it. The Indian had flavored his stew with goose-tongue greens and other wild herbs and the thick beef-steaks were succulent beyond description.

While they ate, Banning and Big Yak conferred at length regarding the present set-up of Circle B's affairs, the Indian's contribution to the discussion being occasional grunts and nods. Banning's talk concerned many things completely foreign to Becky— Tom Romane's untimely death, the progress of Butcherblock's spring round-up as seen riding over from Coulee, and his short but violent meeting with Costaine.

"Anyway, the south section is sewed up," Banning said, turning to the girl across the table. "It's your land, Becky. No matter where you drift from here, you'll have a stake in Circle B, half ownership in all my worldly goods."

At the conclusion of the meal Becky gathered the rude tin dishes into a wreck pan. She heard Banning say something in the Yakima jargon to Big Yak, and saw the Indian strip the upper bunk of its soogans and buffalo robe and head out to the barn with them.

They washed and dried the dishes together and,

having taken care of the necessary chores, found an awkward situation shaping up. It was their first moment of being truly alone.

"You'll sleep yonder," Banning said stiffly, indicating the lower bunk. "Later this week I'll ride over to Medicine Lodge and fetch back some sheets, maybe a mattress to replace that straw tick. The springs are latticed rawhide, but they're tolerable comfortable. Sleep comes easy at this altitude."

Becky seated herself in a chair fashioned of cowhorns cunningly interlaced and covered with a horsehide cushion. She let the warmth of the crackling fire ease the tension in her body, but she could not relax her thoughts.

For the first time since she had exchanged the vows of holy matrimony with this stranger in front of the funny little Baptist minister in Coulee Center, the girl found herself face to face with the reality of a situation which up to now had been something almost apart from her, something that seemed to be happening to someone else.

Her glance shifted over to the bunk. It was wider than a cot, obviously built for two. The upper bunk, where Big Yak had apparently slept, was stripped to its straw tick.

"Reckon you'll want to turn in early," Banning said, squatting on his bootheels in front of the hearth and packing a briar pipe from a copper humidor. "Don't mind the strange noises you'll hear in the night. Lots of varmints prowl these hills, and one coyote can sound like fifty, bayin' at the moon." He paused, clearing his throat, not looking at her. "You lock the door by slipping that hickory pin under the latch."

He lighted his pipe with a sliver from the fire, the glow lining his strong profile with gold. When he had his smoke going he stood up, stretching comfortably.

He was thinking, "She looks pretty even in those pants of Auggie Linklater's damned if she don't." Aloud, he said, "I'm hopin' you'll feel like singing tomorrow, Becky. I reckon you got the nicest voice this side of the angels."

He walked slowly to the door then, pausing for a final glance at her diminutive figure, feet tucked under her, the firelight playing on the classic lines of her face.

"Good night, Becky," he said, and before she could answer he had stepped out into the night and she heard the musical tinkle of his spur chains as he headed out to the barn.

Long after the big pine log had fallen to glowing ash in the hearth, the rustic cabin confined the strange sound of Becky's soft weeping as she lay on the bunk, giving way at last to all the emotional pressures she had kept bottled up inside her since the night of her precipitate flight from Seattle.

She went to sleep without giving thought to bolting the door of the cabin.

FIFTEEN

Banning was in saddle by daylight, having shared a make-shift breakfast out in the harness shed from provisions stocked in the small chuck wagon he and Big Yak took with them on trips up the Gap, overnight from the ranch.

There was more wire to string on the drift fence in anticipation of Butcherblock's arrival in the not far distant future, claim notices to post in compliance with federal law along the boundaries of the south section; a horse to shoe, a milk cow to dehorn and countless other odd jobs around a working ranch.

It was approaching noon when Wes Banning rode back to the ranch, Big Yak being up the Gap chousing young stuff out of the side canyons and corraling them for branding.

Riding in, Banning was alarmed to see a lathered saddle horse ground-hitched outside his door. He spurred into a quick gallop, loosening his six-shooter in holster, and his eyes were round-sprung with tension when he dismounted and ran to the door.

Had Costaine sent a gunhawk out to Circle B so soon?

But it was Paul Priggee who was seated at the table eating a slab of dried apricot pie which Becky had baked that morning.

"Howdy," Banning said, his voice showing the anti-climax that was in him, his eyes as they touched

Becky's glowing with relief at finding her safe. "You had me spooked. Guess I shouldn't leave Becky alone this way."

The land agent's seamed face was gravely alert as he shook hands with Banning.

"You can probably guess it took something pretty important to bring me over from Coulee a-hossback at my age, Wes," the oldster said without preliminaries. "Costaine knows the claim you made in Mrs. Banning's name is invalid. He checked with the preacher and knows you weren't married at the time my records showed you filed on the south section."

Banning's face drained of color. In the back of his head he had considered this chink in their armor, wondered if Greg Costaine would be sharp enough to spot it.

"If this means you'll face an investigation, Paul," he said tensely, "I deserve to be horse-whipped."

Priggee broke into a grin.

"I've covered my tracks, son. I burned all the records relating to your wife's homestead allotment, the ones Costaine might want to force me to produce in court. Costaine will have no whit of written proof that we committed, shall we say, perjury with intent to defraud the federal government."

Banning scowled. "Then Section 33 is still open to filing?"

Priggee reached inside his brushpopper jumper and drew out a folded document.

"Exactly. I'm surprised Costaine didn't think of that before he left, but he didn't. So—I have brought out a new set of papers, which will show that your wife filed claim to Section 33 by due process of law on this day and date, at which time she had been your legal spouse for two days."

Banning threw back his head and laughed.

"Paul, you're sharp as a tomahawk."

"However," Priggee went on in a more serious tone, "I have an equally important reason for riding over here today. Did you stop to remember that Butcherblock can throw its cattle into Chinook Gap by by-passing the mouth of the valley and entering through any one of a dozen side canyons in the north or south rims?"

Banning said confidently, "But I leased every inch of ground inside the surveyed limits of the Gap. That lease has four years to run. If Butcherblock tries to invade my graze I would have a legal right to defend my rights with force."

Priggee nodded. "Apparently you have forgotten the stipulations of your contract with the government, my friend. The law is explicit on one point. Any rancher leasing public graze must within twelve calendar months from date of entry, graze a minimum of one animal for every twenty acres of leased graze. In your case that would amount to twenty-five hundred head. I see by your tally book that you are running considerably short of a thousand head at this time—the cattle you bought last summer from Jim Showalter."

Banning's mouth went slack. "But that stipulation is just so much red tape, Paul. You know it's a technicality. To keep small outfits from sewing up more than their share of grazing and timber lands. The minimum restriction clause is never enforced."

Priggee said, "The fact that there is no precedent for such enforcement doesn't mean that Greg Costaine's lawyers in Medicine Lodge won't spot that loophole and take advantage of it, Wes."

Banning's shoulder slumped. "Why didn't you remind me of this the other night?"

"I assumed you had your herd built up to the required minimum. The anniversary of your lease comes due in only four days, Wes."

Banning's eyes filled with a slow anguish as he pondered this latest bombshell to his hopes.

"If Costaine puts his herd into the Gap, you figure the courts will throw out my suit for trespass, then?"

"I'd hate to gamble in your favor, son."

Across the table, Becky sensed the despair growing in her husband and felt an acute sympathy sweep her being, knowing something of the disaster Priggee's information meant to him.

"Unless you've got a full twenty-five hundred head of stock grazing on Gap grass within the next four days," Priggee said earnestly, "you can expect Butcherblock to move in."

Banning nodded. "With enough cattle to ruin the Gap before the courts could grant an injunction against Costaine," he said. "It looks like Costaine holds the aces, Paul."

Becky spoke up hesitantly, "Isn't there some way you could bring in extra cattle to meet the government obligation before your deadline expires, Wes?"

Banning stared at the girl abstractly. "Cattle cost money. I got barely enough cash to keep us in grub over the summer, Becky. I'm in debt for the six hundred head under my brand as it is. I—wait a minute!"

Banning straightened up, his glance shuttling from his wife to Paul Priggee and back again.

"You've given me an idea, Becky," he said excitedly. "Jim Showalter's hard up for grass on Lazy S—I saw that riding through yesterday. Paul, what's to prevent me from rigging up an undercover deal with Showalter—have three thousand or so head of Lazy S beef into the Gap before the lease deadline expires next Thursday—and produce a fake bill of sale to show Costaine?"

Priggee's sad spaniel eyes took on a keen sparkle.

"There's your answer, son. Have Showalter give you a bill of sale with the private understanding that title to his stock actually remains with Lazy S. Showalter has plenty of reason to hate Costaine's guts. He'd do it."

Big Yak made his unobtrusive entrance into the cabin at this moment. Banning wheeled to face the Indian and said, "Yak, saddle the appaloosa stud for me. I'm riding over to Lazy S this afternoon."

As the Indian turned to the door, Banning held him with a gesture. He turned to Priggee.

"When do you have to get back to Coulee, Paul?"

The old man shrugged. "This is Sunday, you know. I'll have to open the office tomorrow. Be in the saddle most of the night as it is, Wes."

Banning turned back to the Indian. "Yak, I want you

to leave your other work and stick around the ranch until I get back. Don't get out of earshot of my squaw at any time, day or night. Understand?"

Becky spoke up quickly, "But I know how much work Big Yak has lined up, Wes. I'm not afraid to stay by myself. I know how to use a gun, if you're afraid Mr. Costaine might show up, or somebody from Madam Bartreau's."

It was the first allusion she had made to her past, and she bit her lip, glancing quickly to see if her slip of the tongue had registered on either of the men.

"Me guard squaw," Big Yak promised, and went out.

Banning stepped over to the table to sign the new homestead application the agent had brought him. After Becky had put her signature to the document, she said, "If you're leaving at once, you must eat, Wes. I've got dinner warming in the oven—"

As Banning wolfed down his food, too absorbed in his immediate plans to notice that the girl had accomplished miracles with her crude utensils and the scanty provender available, Paul Priggee spoke another word of warning.

"Bear in mind, Wes, that if Butcherblock gets wind of a trail drive from Showalter's range, he'll hit you with everything he's got. Costaine's Texas gunfighters will get a chance to earn the fighting pay Costaine gives them to take care of just such an emergency as this one."

"Thanks, Paul," Banning said humbly. "I don't reckon there's any way I can ever repay you for what you've done."

Priggee chuckled. "You might name your first boy after me," he said.

Banning stared at Becky, saw the deep color rise in her cheeks at Priggee's joking remark. He felt a sudden pain go through him, a feeling that he had placed a wonderful girl in a shabby position, thinking only of his own selfish interests.

When it came time to leave, Becky accompanied Banning out to where Big Yak was holding the saddled appaloosa, the fastest mount in Banning's personal string.

"I'm leaving my rifle," Banning said, swinging into stirrups and looking down at the girl. "You can trust Yak completely. I ought to be back inside of three days, with Showalter's help on the trail drive. Meanwhile, I want you to stick close to the cabin. I've already had one run-in with Costaine's gunslingers."

Becky looked up at him, her eyes filled with a shining tenderness that added to Banning's self-condemnation. He had treated her like an unwanted guest up to now, he thought, and an impulse went through him to lean from saddle and kiss her, an impulse which he at once curbed. He thought, She married me to hide out from something or somebody. We've got a deal and no romance goes with it . . .

"I'll pray for you to have luck at Mr. Showalter's, Wes," she said. "Please don't worry about me."

He lifted his Stetson gravely, curvetted the appaloosa stud away from her side and, with a final wave to Paul Priggee standing in the door of his cabin, spurred into a gallop, heading north eastward toward Showalter's Lazy S.

Tears filled Becky's lashes as she walked slowly back to the cabin. Paul Priggee waited in the doorway, his rheumy eyes fixed on the dwindling figure of Wes Banning.

The old man said, "I brought the Seattle papers out with me, Mrs. Banning. Didn't want to mention it while Wes was around, not knowing what your situation is here."

She stared at him, knowing he knew her secret.

"Your picture is prominently displayed in the P.I.," he said. "Everyone in Coulee Center who saw you sing at the Casino the other night knows you're not from Montana, Rebecca."

Instinctively loving and trusting this kindly old public servant, Rebecca Mullinary Banning stepped into the shelter of Priggee's embrace.

"Do you think—anyone in Coulee—will get in touch with my step-father?" she faltered. "I was so sure I would be safe here on Circle B—"

Priggee said with a paternal anguish in his voice, "Your—the man you didn't marry—is offering a thousand dollars cash reward for information leading to your whereabouts, Mrs. Banning. Of course, being of legal age, and married to Wes Banning, you couldn't be forced to leave Circle B."

"I—I want to stay on Circle B—forever, Mr. Priggee," she choked out finally. "But Wes—Wes is building this ranch for somebody else. He doesn't need me, doesn't really want me—"

Priggee held her close, whispering against her ear, "He will, Rebecca. Give him time. If you love him, he'll never know it unless you let him see it in your actions and words. Show Wes what he means to you and he'll never let you go—"

SIXTEEN

Mid-afternoon found Wes Banning crossing the grazed-out sage flats of Butcherblock's north range, in sight of Jim Showalter's line fence.

Remembering from yesterday that Lazy S was out in the foothills branding calves, Banning had not wasted time riding to Showalter's headquarters on the Coulee Center stage road. For several hours now he had seen a thin smudge of dust rising like smoke from Jackpine Valley, leased to Lazy S, and he believed that marked the location of his friend's round-up.

Jim Showalter was one of the few small-tally ranchers who had defied Greg Costaine's expanding authority. During the years Banning had worked as a Butcherblock hand, he had been aware of the state of truce existing between Costaine and his neighbors.

One by one, Butcherblock had absorbed those lesser outfits. Some by purchase. Others by rustling raids which Costaine laid on Indian renegades; the pot-shooting of line riders, murders which could never be directly traced to Costaine. But Foothill County guessed at what it could not prove. Why else would Greg Costaine have imported Texans with notched guns on their belts, gradually replacing his original Montana crew, of which Banning had been one?

Banning's friendship for Jim Showalter had come after his row with foreman Chet Lattimer over grazing methods and his subsequent ousting from the Butcherblock bunkhouse. For a few weeks after that, Banning had worked for Jim Showalter. Then, at Donna Fleming's urging, he had homesteaded at the mouth of the Gap and started his own outfit. Proving up on his section was a simple matter of erecting a cabin and sinking a well and cultivating a few acres of pasture. But it took land and cattle to make a ranch out of a homestead, and Jim Showalter had come forward with a helping hand within a week after Banning got his patent.

He had sold Banning five hundred and fifty head of shorthorns, which had enabled Banning to lease the fifty thousand acres of Chinook Gap graze adjacent to his homestead. Showalter had accepted a token down-payment and Banning's note for the balance. With the exception of the past year's increase, every Hereford inside Banning's drift fence bore a Lazy S iron, vented with the Circle B.

It was a business arrangement, on the surface, but it went deeper than that, Showalter's stocking Circle B's range. Jim Showalter saw in Banning a potential ally in his never-ending fight against Greg Costaine's Butcherblock. Circle B, in the military sense, protected Showalter's vulnerable flank. The sale of beef to the Territory's Indian reservations—largest in America—would enable Banning to eventually pay off his debts and accrued interest.

Knowing the depth of Showalter's friendship, Banning believed the old stockman would be willing to furnish enough cattle to fulfil the technical requirements of his lease. Showalter might even regard the arrangement as a favor to him, for grass conditions were not good on Lazy S this year. Showalter ran about six thousand head of stock on his limited range. If half that number could get summer graze in Chinook Gap, it would relieve Lazy S's home shortage as well as plugging up the legal loophole which Priggee believed Costaine would use to gain entry to the Gap.

These things were milling in Banning's head as he kept his appaloosa at a steady lope, beelining over Costaine's desolate land toward the site of Showalter's round-up in Jackpine Valley.

From his own immediate ranch problems his thoughts turned to the recent cataclysm in his personal affairs. The remembered hurt of finding Donna Fleming in the arms of a cheap tinhorn gambler, and the break-up of their engagement, no longer rankled Banning's pride.

That surprised him, for during the past three years every plan he had made, every dream he had dreamed was focussed on Donna Fleming.

Alone with his thoughts, Banning found himself overwhelmed by the change in his fortunes. His fantastic wedding to a honkytonk singer of whom he knew less than nothing, a girl with a brooding secret of her own, came to fill his thoughts to such an extent that it took the edge off the constant wariness which he invariably practiced when necessity forced him to travel on land controlled by Costaine.

He was putting the appaloosa up a scabrock-terraced ridge when a sudden whicker from the animal caused him to break out of his thoughts with a start. Looking up against the brassy skyline, he saw two men sitting their horses there, watching his approach, the westering sunlight glinting off Winchester carbines balanced across swellfork pommels.

"Butcherblock," he muttered, jerking erect in saddle. He remembered now that he had left his own rifle back at the cabin, for Becky's protection. He had no doubt but that these men waiting like a pair of vultures up there on the ridge crest were Costaine's. Perhaps they had been scouting Chinook Gap, waiting for a chance to catch him away from his own ranch. There was something sinister and predatory about the way in which those silhouetted riders waited as his horse labored up the rocky slope.

The six-gun at his hip was nullified by the longer range of those waiting Winchesters. Under ordinary circumstances Banning would have had no particular apprehension about running across any of his former bunkhouse mates from Butcherblock.

But things were no longer the same on this range. His own stature as a neutral rancher on the outskirts of Costaine's territory had changed the instant his fist had smashed down the cattle baron in Becky's dressing room at the Casino. Banning had no doubt but that Costaine had issued orders to all the Texas owlhooters in his pay to shoot him on sight if the set-up was right. And this situation was made to order for bushwhack murder.

Banning's jaw set in a harsh line as he kept his stud moving up the slope. His right arm hung alongside his cantle rim within easy reach of his gun. He kept the appaloosa head-on to the waiting pair, presenting as narrow a target as possible. There were no roundabout boulders or draws where a man could dive to shelter and put this meeting on a more even basis. As it was he was caught in the open like a sitting quail.

Banning was twenty yards from the ridge crest when he recognized who he was running into. Tex Karnhizel was the rawboned hombre on the buckskin to his left. The big buckaroo with him was Chet Lattimer, foreman in charge of all the working ranches which made up Costaine's tight-knit syndicate.

Neither Karnhizel nor Lattimer made any sign of greeting as the dust of Banning's approach drifted up to them on the sluggish wind. Their mouths were set in anticipatory grins as Banning drew rein on the level hump of the ridge. He felt as alone as if he were in a crater on the moon.

Banning's eyes slid from Karnhizel to Lattimer. Neither spoke, neither moved. They were waiting like spiders poised to spring on a web-caught fly.

Then Karnhizel reached up his left hand to tug the lobe of his ear, a mannerism Banning remembered from his meeting with the Texan the morning of the fence-cutting episode. Karnhizel's right hand was holding his cocked rifle, trigger finger thrust through the brass guard, so that the Winchester could be aimed and fired single-handed.

Lattimer now lifted his .45-70 so the butt plate rested on his knee, barrel pointed skyward.

Hard to tell which was the deadlier of the two. There was no doubting this was a gun trap. The burning, reptilian intensity of their stares told Banning that. The puzzle was why they had not bushwhacked him when he was crossing the lower flats.

He thought wildly, They want to find out something from me before they smoke me down. Or maybe Costaine wants me alive, so he can make me crawl . . .

"Howdy, Wes." Chet Lattimer broke the brittle silence. "How come the bridegroom is drifting loose so soon after the weddin'? Or is your Montany Meadowlark only good for singin'?"

Lattimer's insult put a crazed anger in Banning, but he held his tongue. Karnhizel's .30-30 had swung around now so that its black bore covered Banning. The Texas gunhawk was still stroking his ear, waiting. Lattimer was grinning, the harsh sunshine bringing out the Indian in him. He might have been a Comanche warrior in feather bonnet and war paint, with a scalping knife or a tomahawk in his hand.

"It's a shame yore honkytonk bride is wanted by the law," Lattimer said. "Because she's goin' to have enough trouble without findin' herself a new widow in the bargain."

SEVENTEEN

Banning controlled the rage that Lattimer's drawl kindled in him. That was what the half-breed was trying to do: provoke him into attempting a draw so Karnhizel could bullet-dump him from saddle and they could tell the sheriff over in Coulee they had shot in self defense.

"Leave the girl out of this," Banning snapped. "You aim to give me the same medicine you doled out to the other ranchers who wouldn't quit. What are you two waitin' for? Reinforcements?"

Lattimer's Indianlike face twisted. Tex Karnhizel stirred in his saddle, muttering impatiently, "Say when, *companero.*"

Lattimer shook his head, spurring forward until he was alongside Banning's nigh stirrup. The move boxed their victim between them. The pattern of this set-up was evident now. Karnhizel would fire the pay-off shot. He was leaving the talking to Lattimer.

"Wes, you always been too big for your britches," the Butcherblock foreman said casually. "That's why I had to tie the can to your tail when you worked for Butcherblock. You played your cards the wrong way when you cut loose from Costaine, hombre. If you'd been smart you might have landed a ramrod's job on the Goose Crick ranch. Costaine was thinking about it."

"Why the palaver, Chet?" Karnhizel growled testily.

Banning said harshly, "Quit stalling, Chet. What are you leading up to?"

Lattimer cuffed back his rawhide-laced Stetson and regarded Banning thoughtfully. "Your fancy plans in Coulee didn't pan out color the other night, Wes. Did you know that claim you got to the south section ain't worth the ink Priggee wasted on it?"

Banning said, "Meaning you found out Becky filed on it before she was actually my wife, Chet?"

"So you know. I'm surprised you'd be that careless, kid, after all the trouble you went to." Lattimer glanced toward Karnhizel, who had brought his left hand down to steady his carbine muzzle now. A nod from Lattimer would bring a pointblank slug to knock him from saddle, Banning knew.

"Chet, I ain't as careless as Costaine might think," he said. "It so happens I filed another claim—a valid one, this time—to that section. Only this morning."

What Banning had disclosed roused Lattimer's curiosity to the extent that he held off his fatal signal to Karnhizel.

"For a man who is as good as dead, you don't lie very well, kid."

Banning shrugged. "I've got the bona fide claim papers in my saddlebag, Lattimer. Priggee rode out from Coulee yesterday to fix 'em up, to cover himself as well as to block Costaine's play when he brings his herd up to the Gap. My being dead won't alter that, Lattimer. If you shove your herd across Becky's homestead, Paul Priggee will see that Uncle Sam slaps the hooks on Costaine for violation of federal law."

100

Lattimer reached out, rubbing thumb and fingers together.

"Let's have a look at this paper of yours," he sneered. "I can't see an old gaffer like Priggee takin' the trouble to ride ninety miles to help out a saloon wench. Priggee's got sense enough to know you're living on borrowed time even if you ain't."

Banning twisted in saddle, leaning back to unbuckle a saddlebag. Rummaging in it, he fished out a folded sheet of yellow paper. It was the duplicate of the original claim Priggee had filled out that night in Coulee, and which Banning had stuffed into the saddle pouch for safekeeping.

Without straightening up Banning passed the paper to Lattimer, who had to hold his rifle and bridle reins in his left hand in order to take the document.

Through the tail of his eye Banning saw that Karnhizel's attention had shifted to his foreman, as Lattimer shook the paper open to examine it. In the act of bringing himself back to an upright position in the saddle, Banning's right arm had to brush over his gun butt, hidden from Karnhizel's view.

It was a totally innocent-appearing shift of position, and the fact that Banning kept his head turned toward Lattimer further served to maneuver Karnhizel off guard.

Banning's move was swift and sure, rehearsed a moment before. He had everything to win and nothing to lose by this gamble.

Snatching the .45 from leather and bringing his arm up to clear his own saddle pommel, Banning squeezed off his shot before Karnhizel caught the glint of gun-metal in Banning's fist.

The slug smashed Karnhizel in the shoulder and the drilling impact of the two-ounce missile sent the Texan cartwheeling out of saddle, his Winchester exploding automatically as the slug of lead caused him to jerk trigger.

Banning felt the shock of Karnhizel's slug catching his appaloosa in the skull. He knew his horse was going down and he kicked his boots free of the oxbows.

Acrid fumes from his own gun boiled about his face. Less than a clock-tick of time had elapsed since Lattimer had shaken the paper open to read it. Now Karnhizel's buckskin was wheeling in panic and galloping off down the north face of the hill, the Texan's right boot caught in a tapaderoed stirrup, dragging the man along the ground like a sack of carrion.

The wind whipped the paper away as Lattimer vented a yell and tried to get his carbine into the play. He was too late. The black muzzle of Banning's fuming gun covered him now and Lattimer knew he was as good as dead.

But unaccountably, Banning held his second shot. With his free hand he grabbed the ring of Lattimer's bridle bit before the horse could bolt.

"Raise 'em!" Banning yelled, dimly aware of his own appaloosa toppling inertly to the ground. "Drop the rifle—"

Lattimer's Winchester hit the rocks on the opposite

side of his horse, which had started to buck and would have bolted had it not been for Banning's weight on the headstall.

Trying to keep his seat, the Butcherblock foreman knocked off his Stetson as his arms lifted, pure panic in his yellow eyes.

"All right, step down."

When Lattimer swung out of stirrups, his back to Banning in the process, the Circle B man reached out to hook his six-gun under the curved walnut stock of Lattimer's sidearm and flipped it from holster, the gun landing in the weeds beyond the carcass of Banning's dead horse.

Thus unheeled, Lattimer turned to face Banning, his arms raised.

Incredibly, all this had happened in a time span of less than ten seconds. Now Tex Karnhizel was being dragged to sure death as the buckskin stampeded down the hillslope. Karnhizel's rifle, lodged in a heap of weeds marking a section corner, was still smoking from the blast which had accidentally found its target on Banning's mount.

Further along the ridge, a vagrant dust-devil picked up the paper Banning had taken from his saddle pouch and was whirling it up into the sky.

"Go ahead and shoot, damn you!" Lattimer panted. "You've been honing for this chance long enough. If you think I'm going to crawl—"

Banning grunted shortly, "I ought to kill you, half-breed. But I want to send you back to Smoky Butte where Costaine is waiting for word that I've been dry-gulched."

A semblance of self-control returned to Lattimer now.

"You're loco, Wes. If you think—"

"Peel off your boots, Chet. I've got plans for you."

Lattimer stared, not comprehending. "What?" he said.

"Take off your boots. Likewise your shirt and pants."

Trembling visibly, Lattimer hopped around on one leg while he tugged off a spike-heeled Justin.

"Wes, you wouldn't stake me out to an anthill—"

"An attractive prospect, Lattimer, but I ain't no Injun. No. I'm just sending you back to Butcherblock, mother-naked as a skinned rabbit."

Horror began to kindle in the ramrod's eyes as he peeled off his shirt and waist overalls, and then, prodded by the ominous double click of Banning's six-gun hammer, divested himself of his under drawers and socks.

Standing there stripped to his skin, Lattimer had time to consider the appalling prospect ahead of him. The nearest Butcherblock camp was at the Goose Creek ranch, twenty miles distant. Not only the physical ordeal of that trek rose to confound Lattimer now. A thing like this couldn't be kept secret. Word of his disgrace would travel until he was the laughingstock of the county . . .

Banning gestured toward the south.

"Start walkin', Chester. Watch out for rattlesnakes and sharp rocks. Reckon you won't be too sunburned before night comes on, with the mosquitoes and such."

Lattimer groaned.

"You'll let me take my horse—"

"What'll I ride on—this carcass Karnhizel shot? Get started, son, before I take pity on you and blow your brains out."

Lattimer's throat worked, but he made no further remonstrance. He started picking his way across the abrasive rubble like a cat walking on hot bricks, his tawny flesh already beginning to show pink from the scorching sun.

Twenty torturous yards down the slope, Lattimer turned to see that Banning had gathered all his clothing into a little pile and was touching a match to them, using cigarette papers to get his fire started. There would be no returning for his boots.

When Lattimer's clothing was well ablaze, Banning stripped his saddle from the dead appaloosa and swapped it with Lattimer's. He collected Lattimer's six-gun and rifle, along with Karnhizel's Winchester, and left them in a neat pile by the saddle, after taking the precaution of removing the cylinder from the six-shooter and the magazines and breech loads from the rifles.

By the time he was ready to ride, Banning saw that Lattimer was plodding along the smooth sandy bottom of a small gulch. A shudder touched Banning's spine, thinking of the shape Chet Lattimer would be in before he crossed that desert. His feet would be bloody and crippled, his hide thorn-torn and insect bitten.

Against the chance of starting a prairie fire, Banning

doused the smouldering clothes with water from his canteen. Then, with a final glance in the direction of the pitiful figure of Chet Lattimer, Banning mounted and resumed his ride northward.

EIGHTEEN

Karnhizel's buckskin gelding was grazing in some weeds along the Lazy S boundary fence. A quarter of a mile back Banning had located the mangled corpse of the Texas outlaw. Karnhizel's skull had been reduced to pulp by iron-shod hoofs. It gave Banning some small measure of comfort to know that his hasty shot had not killed Karnhizel outright.

He located a gate where the Medicine Lodge wagon road crossed Showalter's fence, and sundown overtook him at the east mouth of Jackpine Valley, where Showalter's round-up crew was working.

Full dark had come to the valley by the time Banning located the flare of the Lazy S cookfire. When he was close enough to make out the silhouettes of Showalter's men around the chuckwagon he sent a cautious halloo toward the camp.

The cook answered his hail and, suddenly recalling that he was forking a horse bearing the enemy's brand, Banning dismounted and walked up to the camp, being careful to identify himself from a distance.

Relief flowed through him as white-haired Jim Showalter bowlegged out to greet him. Almost before they shook hands, the Lazy S boss spotted the

Butcherblock iron on the horse Banning was leading.

"You gone back to work for Costaine?" Showalter asked harshly.

"Hardly," Banning laughed. "This is Chet Lattimer's stud. Borrowed it after him and Tex Karnhizel cornered me coming over this afternoon."

Showalter's eyes narrowed. "You tangled with Lattimer and Karnhizel and came out of it with a whole hide and a Butcherblock nag?"

Banning grinned, noting that the Lazy S punchers were listening to the by-play.

"Yep. Karnhizel got stirrup-drug a way, so he's buzzard bait now. I sent Mister Lattimer back home, minus his clothes. Stark, mother-naked. He cut a fine figger of manhood, tip-toeing off through the cactus. Looked like the Injun he is."

Howls of immoderate laughter swept the ranks of Showalter's crew. Banning accepted a tin cup of coffee and a plate of barbecued meat and spuds and sourdough biscuits and hunkered down by the chuckwagon to eat. The crew was still laughing when Banning started rolling his after-supper cigarette.

Most of the crew, wearied from a long day in the saddle, sought the comfort of their bedrolls, making ribald comments about the present status of Lattimer's homeward journey in the raw. Not until he and Jim Showalter were alone by the dying campfire did Banning explain his reason for riding over from Circle B.

Showalter listened impassively but with a keen interest as Banning brought him up to date on his affairs.

"So what I need to copper Costaine's next bet is the loan of around three thousand head of your feeder stock, Jim," Banning concluded. "To make it look good I'll have to be able to show Costaine your bill of sale, proving I have met the government's minimum requirements for holding leased public land. All you'll get out of it is a trail drive out of season, I'm afraid, and good summer graze for half of your beef."

Showalter twirled his sandy mustache with a stub of forefinger he had lost to a dallied rope in his youth.

"You got only three days to do it in?" the old rancher commented. "Shavin' it perty fine, but I reckon we can do it."

Banning stared at the glowing coals, grinning.

"You can see what a tight crack it'll put Costaine's tail in when he sees he can't run those twelve thousand head in the Gap," he pointed out. "Butcherblock's range is cut to the bedrock, as bad as if he'd been sheeped out. I understand the grass ain't worth a damn down Yakima way. Which means Costaine will have to drive his herd all the way to eastern Oregon or face a die-off."

A silent chuckle shook Showalter's stooped shoulders.

"Hell, son, I'd be willin' to donate you three thousand head, just for the fun of crowdin' Costaine out on the end of a limb. You realize this could even bankrupt Butcherblock?"

Banning realized that his mission to Lazy S had paid off. Any last lingering doubt as to whether Showalter would see eye to eye with him on a wholesale transfer of cattle from his home range to Circle B had been dispelled.

"It'll take us two days to haze your beef over to the Gap," Banning said soberly. "I figure Costaine will have his herd up to my fence by the morning of the third day. Any little thing like a coyote stampedin' us would ruin the deal."

Showalter poked a sagebrush twig into the dying coals.

"We better play it safe and move by night," he said. "It'll take some hustling, but I can round up a good three thousand head right here in Jackpine tomorrow. Shovin' those critters over to the Gap by night won't give some cruisin' Butcherblock hand a chance to spot our dust and get wise to what we're doin'."

An hour later, stretched out on a tarp under borrowed soogans from the Lazy S hoodlum wagon, Wes Banning stared up at the star-powdered Washington sky and let his thoughts drift back to Becky.

He stirred restlessly in his blankets, recalling Chet Lattimer's cryptic words: *"Yore honkytonk bride is wanted by the law."*

Where had Lattimer got his information? What was back of Becky's eagerness to hide herself on Circle B as his wife? Some powerful motive must have impelled her to place herself at the mercy of a total stranger, marrying him with the full knowledge that he might ignore his pledge to keep the marriage on a strictly impersonal basis.

On the ragged edge of drifting off to sleep, Wes Banning doubted if he would ever learn the answers to the enigma of his wife's past life. He only knew that Becky was married to him and therefore deserving of his protection and his good faith. The fact that she did not love him, probably could never love him, did not alter his moral responsibility to her.

NINETEEN

The next forty-eight hours found Wes Banning too busy with lass' rope and peg pony to give a thought to Becky's mystery. A trail herd had to be bunched in the upper end of Jackpine Valley, a task which imposed a superhuman burden on Showalter's tough crew.

By the end of the following day, Showalter's tally showed slightly more than twenty five hundred head of Lazy S stuff had been choused out of the brushy ravines facing the valley.

Tired as they were, Showalter's loyal crew, top hands from foreman to wrangler, did no grumbling over the prospect of starting a night drive. They knew it was their best insurance against drawing Greg Costaine's army of gun-fighters over from Butcherblock to thwart Banning's move to stock Chinook Gap to the minimum regulations of the public grazing law.

It was a moonless night, which was to their advantage. Another factor in their favor was that the narrowing flanks of Jackpine Valley kept their herd compact in a mile-long column, and shielded their westward passage from discovery by any random Butcherblock rider.

At dawn of the second day they bedded the herd at the timbered box end of the valley. Exhaustion sent every man to his bedroll with the bare minimum of herd guards to take turns keeping the trail-gaunted cattle from drifting into the timber.

Banning, riding to the high ridge overlooking Jackpine Valley on the south, returned to the noon camp with the report that Costaine had his huge pool herd on the move. The fact that the sun was obscured by a mushrooming pall of dust lifting off the outer desert had already tipped off Showalter as to the probability that Butcherblock was marching on Circle B's approaches.

"Reckon Costaine will bed down his herd on the Beaver Crick bottoms tonight," Banning opined. "The anniversary date of my leasing the Gap is tonight at midnight. Costaine figgers he can cut my drift fence and haze across my wife's south section, unless Lattimer has reached him with what I told him about Priggee drawing up new papers."

Showalter said dubiously, "Too bad you showed Lattimer your hole card, son."

"Had to, to draw Karnhizel's eye off my shirt buttons at the time, Jim."

The Lazy S boss said thoughtfully, "Of course you know Lattimer will be after your scalp for certain, after what you done to him. He'd be laughed off the range if he didn't nail your hide to his bunkhouse door."

Banning showed no particular concern over Showalter's dire forebodings. "Time enough to handle Lattimer when he comes huntin' trouble. It's meeting

Costaine at my drift fence tomorrow morning that keeps me guessin'."

The Lazy S boss said gently, "You won't be playin' solitaire, you know. My boys have wanted a tangle with Butcherblock so bad that I've had to bar 'em from going to Medicine Lodge on nights I knew Butcherblock's boys were in town. My crew will be waitin' at Circle B when Costaine shows up tomorrow."

Banning felt an ache stab through his throat as he met his old friend's steely, reassuring glance. It had not occurred to him to ask Lazy S for manpower to back him. That could easily lead to a bloody shoot-out against overpowering odds. Banning had depended on the moral reinforcement of the government laws to call Costaine's bluff when the showdown came.

"I hardly know what to say, Jim. Your boys got no stake in my troubles. It wouldn't be fair to them."

Showalter laughed. "We ain't doin' this for charity, son. I got a hunch this may be the break we been lookin' for, to bankrupt Costaine. With Chinook Gap closed to him, Costaine will have to hunt grass outside the Territory, like you said. He might find himself heading back to Montana where he come from."

Shortly after dusk the herd was started moving again, this time up over the Jackpine ridge and onto the benchland facing Circle B. By midnight the bulk of the herd was over the hump, boxed in by flank riders, with Showalter's chuck and hoodlum wagons bringing up the drags.

Seeing Chinook Gap's rearing rimrocks forming their black shoulders against the further mountains, Wes Banning searched for the low-hung star which would be Becky's lamp in the windows of his cabin under the North Rim, but all was darkness there.

Somewhere abreast of them to the southward, Costaine's tremendous herd, probably the largest in the annals of the Territory's ranching, was bedded down along the green borders of Beaver Creek, awaiting tomorrow's deadline expiration and the final short push into the Gap.

This next three miles would be risky, if the sound of the bawling cows and clacking hoofs should be carried to the ears of Butcherblock nighthawks. But as long as the wind held from the south . . .

When the Lazy S herd was moving across the flats, Showalter and Wes Banning galloped ahead to open the drift fence where it crossed the creek. The Beaver bottom formed a natural entry into the Gap.

It was still two hours short of daylight when the vanguard of Showalter's herd reached the opening in the fence and began flooding through. Handling the cattle was a relatively simple thing now, for they smelled water and grass and wanted to head toward it.

Day's first pink glow was spilling across the coulee-scarred desert toward the Columbia River basin when the last straggler was hazed through the Circle B fence and the Lazy S wagons parked under the cottonwoods.

The worst was over. Two nights of trail driving had passed without stampede or other delay. Apparently they had made the coup without drawing the attention of any Costaine rider. So far as Banning knew, the presence of nearly three thousand head of extra cattle in the Gap would come to Greg Costaine tomorrow as a total and devastating surprise.

Costaine would think twice before trying to blast his way by force into the Gap. That would be in open violation of federal law, and Costaine had his political future to think about. With Circle B backed by the might of Lazy S guns, a showdown of force from Butcherblock would entail heavy casualties on both sides as well.

The cattle were spreading up the Gap of their own accord, the rimming cliffs doing away with the necessity of herd riders. After a consultation with Showalter at the camp, Banning crossed Beaver Creek and headed toward his Circle B cabin.

He saw Big Yak forking hay to his milk cow out in the corral. A wisp of smoke lifted from the rock chimney, rousing in Banning a mental picture of Becky preparing breakfast for him. The prospect put a physical thrill through him.

Riding in, he lifted echoes with a whooping shout and dismounted in front of the cabin. The slab door was open and Banning strode directly inside, his voice crackling with fatigue as he called, "Becky?"

Silence answered him. He looked around, scowling, and as his eyes became accustomed to the dim light, he was struck by the transformation which his bride had accomplished during his three-day absence.

The floor puncheons were spotlessly scrubbed. Window panes sparkled, washed and polished for the first time since they had been installed. The tin dishes had been scoured until they shone like pewter and had been neatly stacked on a shelf. The rusty stove looked like new under a coat of blacking, its nickel work burnished to a high gloss.

Everywhere was evidence of Becky's work. Gone from the rafters were the years' accumulation of dust and sooty cobwebs. The piles of beaver plews had been taken out. The table was covered with a scrap of bright cloth, neatly hemmed by hand, which Becky must have made from dress material out of her portmanteau.

A warmth ran through Banning which was a totally new sensation to him. Becky, with so little to work with, had transformed this bachelor cabin into a home. He said aloud, "And this was the shack that wasn't good enough for Donna—"

A shadow fell across the doorway and he turned eagerly. But instead of Becky, it was the stolid-faced Big Yak in his greasy buckskins and knee-high legging moccasins, toting his milk pail.

"We done it, Yak," Banning said, knowing his Indian cowhand's interest in his mission to Lazy S. "Better than twenty-nine hundred head of prime beef are going to get fat in the Gap this summer. And Showalter's crew is going to stand by until Costaine shows up."

He stopped talking, reading some hint of tragedy in the Yakima buck's timeless face.

"Yak, where's Becky? Where's my squaw?"

The Indian fumbled inside his beaded jacket and drew out an envelope.

"Your squaw, she gone. Not come back. She tell Yak, give this to boss."

TWENTY

A numb sense of loss put its chill in the pit of Banning's belly as he took the sealed letter from the Indian.

"Becky's gone? When?"

"One sleep. White squaw you call um Donna, she come on cayuse. Squaws make pow-wow, not so skookum. Your squaw cry, like papoose with colic. Send Yak out, make more pow-wow."

Banning dragged a dust-caked sleeve over his eyes, a sick sensation traveling through his nerves.

"Donna Fleming came over from Coulee," he repeated dully, "and took Becky away. But why?"

Yak pointed to the envelope in Banning's hand.

"Yak not know. Yak saddle cayuse for squaw. Squaw say Yak good Injun. Then go. Two squaws go, heap fast, Tillicums."

Moisture made the cowman blink momentarily.

"I might have expected this," he ground out bitterly. "Leastwise Becky served her purpose. She's helped me crimp Costaine's horns."

He groped his way through the door and sat down on a bench, ripping open Becky's letter. Inside it was a single sheet of paper filled with the girl's handwriting, and a clipping torn from a Seattle *Post-Intelligencer* six days old.

Incredulously he read the account of Rebecca Mullinary's disappearance from Seattle on the eve of her wedding to the heir of a wealthy steamship family.

Then, oblivious to the ravening hunger in his belly or the sounds of Big Yak preparing breakfast inside the cabin, he turned his attention to Becky's farewell message:

Dear Wes,

The enclosed newspaper clipping will tell you who I am, but not why I did what I did. Mr. Priggee brought it with him Sunday. Today, Monday, I have had a visit from your ex-fiancée, Miss Fleming. Donna came out to Circle B with the express purpose of warning me that my whereabouts have been telegraphed to my step-father and the Seattle police. She learned that from the telegrapher who sent the message for—can you guess who?—Greg Costaine. He must have seen my picture in the same paper.

Knowing that my presence here is an inconvenience and an embarrassment for you, Wes, I have decided to accompany Miss Fleming back to Coulee Center. She has very graciously offered to lend me the money to get to New York. By the time you read these lines I will be on my way.

Although you have never asked me about myself, I feel that I owe you an explanation, even though we will never meet again. I would not want you to think of me merely as a singer in Madam Bartreau's saloon.

I ran away from Seattle because I could not

endure the thought of becoming the wife of a man who had been three times divorced already. The marriage was something my step-father wanted because a tie-up with a wealthy and influential family would further his ambitions to someday become Washington's governor.

My purpose was to reach New York, where I have relatives of my real father, who would cherish me for myself. I had barely money enough to reach Yakima. While there I saw an advertisement stating that the Paris Casino wanted to hire a singer at fifty dollars a week. Because I majored in Music at the University, I seized this opportunity to try and earn my fare east.

You know what happened in Coulee Center. Your offer of marriage was a straw to snatch at, so I did. Knowing that I have served your purpose and that it would be expecting too much to remain at Circle B, I am therefore taking advantage of Miss Fleming's kindness. Donna loves you, Wes. She told me so. Whatever happened between you is something she regrets.

I shall never forget this fantastic interlude in my life, nor will I ever forget you and your kindness and understanding. Our wedding can of course be annulled, so that you will be free to marry the girl of your choice. I shall pray for your happiness and for Circle B's success in the future. God bless you, Wes, and please do not think unkindly of me for not waiting to tell you all this personally. I could not run the risk of having my step-father

and ex-fiancé find me. I will return your mother's
ring by mail.

Sincerely your friend,
Becky.

A grim smile made its taut fixture on Banning's mouth
as he laid the letter down. Unlike Becky, he took a dim
view of Donna Fleming's sincerity in helping get his
wife out of the Territory. Donna had been impelled by
baser motives than an act of kindness to an unfortunate
woman. Her true reason—

A rider hammered into the ranch grounds at this
moment, bringing Wes Banning to his feet. It was one
of Showalter's drovers.

"He's comin' up the crick toward your gate, Banning!" shouted the Lazy S rider, reining up in a swirl
of dust. "The great lord Costaine himself. And he's got
Sheriff Jeffers with him."

TWENTY-ONE

A cold laugh escaped Banning at the news, a savage
urge for committing physical violence bubbling
uncontrollably through his veins. Becky's running out
on him was completely justified and he felt no censure
toward her for so doing. She owed him nothing. Yet
her leaving would put a scar on his heart, and this
prospect of locking horns with Greg Costaine was the
physical outlet Banning needed.

"Sheriff's with him, eh?" Banning yelled back. "I got

119

just the papers to wipe Jeffers' nose for him—"

He ducked back into the house, a sudden dread striking him that Becky might have taken the homestead papers with her, since they were recorded in her name.

But he found them on the cloth-covered table, weighted down by a brass lamp which the girl had carefully cleaned and polished until it shone like gold.

Jamming the paper in his pocket, Banning raced out to his horse and with the Lazy S cowboy at his stirrup, headed for the Beaver Creek gate at a dead run.

As he neared the creek he saw that Jim Showalter and his heavily-armed riders were fanning out along the drift fence, probably as far as the South Rim. That show of force must have already been spotted by Costaine and the sheriff, who would be at a loss to account for it, knowing that Big Yak was all the crew Banning had.

Banning waved the Lazy S messenger back as he caught sight of Costaine at the open gate, mounted on his flashy white Arabian. With him was Jeffers, the underling who wore the star of Foothill County law, a sheriff bought and paid for by Butcherblock.

Jeffers and Costaine waited at the gate as Banning jogged to a halt before them.

"Mornin', Banning," the sheriff said, rubbing a sleeve on the star pinned to his vest. "Reckon you know why I'm here this mornin'. I don't want Mr. Costaine to have any trouble when he puts his herd across the south section."

Banning shook his head. "Guess again, sheriff. My

wife is the legal owner of that section. You'd be an accessory to violating a federal law if you let Costaine trespass."

Costaine's face was stony as he rapped out, "Your title's not worth a damn, Wes. You weren't married when Paul Priggee took your application. Priggee will serve time for tryin' to pull that sandy for you. I'll see to that."

Banning's brows arched in feigned surprise as he spurred up closer and thrust a paper under Costaine's nose.

"Priggee knew that, Greg, so he fixed up papers that will hold water in court. Look 'em over."

Costaine's iron control wavered as he grabbed the paper, saw that it was a government homestead application, and that it bore a date only three days old.

Realizing he had been out-maneuvered, Costaine lifted his muddy eyes to stare balefully at the Circle B man.

" 'Sta bueno—so you've blocked off the mouth of the Gap to my cattle, Banning. No matter." Costaine turned to the sheriff, who was witnessing this by-play with a bovine stupidity. "Jeff, it looks like I'll have to shove my beef into the Gap from further up the South Rim." He turned back to Banning. "I've kept a close watch on you this past year, my bucko. Under the terms of the federal grazing act, you've got to have a minimum of one cow for every twenty acres of leased land. You miss that by a hell of a margin. Today's the expiration date of the time the government allots a lessee to build up his herd to legal size."

Banning grinned cheerfully. "Well, what do you know?" he said archly. Then his expression changed. "Costaine, I have a whole card to show you. You'll find Circle B is grazing a thousand head over the required minimum. Cattle I bought from Lazy S. Here's Stowalter's bill of sale, dated yesterday, to prove it. I've complied with the grazing regulations and then some."

Greg Costaine's eyes looked sick as he accepted the sheet of tablet paper Banning took out of his shirt pocket. It was a bill of sale stating that, for value received, James Showalter of the Lazy S ranch had transferred title to 2,875 head of beef to Wesley Banning. Date of sale one day prior to the expiration of the Chinook Gap's first year of lease to Circle B . . .

"What's wrong Greg?" Sheriff Jeffers inquired anxiously.

Costaine passed the bill of sale over to the sheriff. His face held the blank look of a steer stunned by a pole axe as his glance strayed across the creek to study Showalter's line of gunhung Lazy S riders, spaced at hundred-yard angles along the Circle B drift fence.

Sheriff Jeffers coughed apologetically. "Greg, it looks like Banning has out-foxed you. My hands are tied. I'm checkin' the bet to you."

Banning reached to accept the spurious bill of sale from Jeffers. He knew that this moment was the nadir of Costaine's life, the first time he had ever been face to face with defeat.

"You got a lot of hungry cattle losing tallow on

you," Banning grinned, enjoying this moment. "You better start thinkin' where you can find range you haven't ruined by overgrazing. Oregon might be your best bet, if your stock can stand that long a drive this time of year. You're hooked on your own pitchfork, Costaine, and damned if I don't enjoy watching you wiggle."

Sheriff Jeffers said gruffly, "I can arrest Banning on Lattimer's complaint of assault an' battery if you say so, Greg."

Banning laughed. "Oh—so the ramrod showed up in a bad humor, did he? I never laid a hand on the mangey son. What's wrong with him? Fallen arches, or a bad case of sunburn?"

Greg Costaine picked up his reins and turned on Jeffers with a savage oath.

"Lattimer can handle his own complaints, Jeff. Let's get the hell out of here."

The Butcherblock boss wheeled his magnificent white Arab and jabbed its flank with his gut-hooks, Jeffers wheeling to follow him. Over his shoulder Costaine flung back a choked shout:

"You win this pot, Wes. But the game ain't over by a damned sight. Laugh while you can, son."

As the two riders pounded off in the direction of the Butcherblock herd being held down the creek a few miles to the eastward, Banning heard the faint sound of cheering from Showalter and his Lazy S crew, who had witnessed Costaine's galling defeat from beyond Beaver Creek.

This should have been the crowning hour of Banning's life. He had just reaped the harvest of a long and gruelling feud against Costaine's power and arrogance. But the victory left him cold, empty, wrung dry by the anticlimax of it.

He groaned aloud, "Becky, if you'd only stayed long enough to share this with me, made it worth the celebrating—"

A wild impulse seized him to ride to Coulee Center and overtake her. But that was useless, considering the time element. Becky had probably boarded the Concord which left the county seat at daylight yesterday morning. By now she would be on a train headed for Walla Walla and the east. There was no hope of even dispatching a telegram from the Medicine Lodge station and begging her to reconsider her decision to leave the West.

All unknowingly, Becky Banning was leaving a void in him, taking something precious from him that he would never replace. As suddenly as that, Wes Banning knew that all he counted worthwhile in life was wrapped up in his love for Becky. A love which he himself had not felt burgeoning into life, a love he had never put into words and which Becky would not have accepted even if he had known in time . . .

TWENTY-TWO

Becky turned away from the ticket window of the Coulee Center stage office, her heart constricted by a nameless sense of frustration as she realized the meaning of the agent's words.

The weekly stage for Wenatchee had left yesterday morning at five. This was Friday morning at nine. The agent had said there would not be another stage making connections with the overland railroad at Wenatchee until next Thursday.

"If it's powerful important, ma'am," the ticket seller's voice broke through her daze, "you might hire Cy Crowfant to drive you south in a livery buggy. That's about all the help I can offer you."

Becky set down her portmanteau and dabbed at her eyes with a handkerchief. She turned to face the bearded man behind the wicket.

"When—when do you expect a stage in that made connections with the train from Seattle, sir?"

She flushed, knowing that the express company agent knew her sordid story and must have guessed the reason for the urgency in her voice. She knew that her step-father—or worse yet, her jilted fiancé—would be arriving in Coulee Center on the first available transportation.

"Reckon that would be the six-forty stage that got in from the south this mornin', ma'am."

Becky steeled herself to glean more information.

"Did—did anyone get off the stage—a man who might have inquired about my whereabouts?"

The agent averted his eyes, his embarrassment telling her that he understood her question all too well.

"I didn't see who got off, lady. You might ask the hostlers who changed teams for the jehu."

Blinded by her tears, Becky Banning left the stage office and headed for the Elkhorn House. She had shared the hospitality of Donna Fleming's room in the hotel since her arrival here; it had been her refuge while she waited for the first stage out of town.

Climbing the steps of the hostelry, she flinched as she heard a male voice call her by name from down the street.

She wheeled, terror chilling her, and then relaxed as she saw the bent figure of Paul Priggee walking away from the Coulee Center post office, a bundle of mail in his hand.

Becky had not contacted the land agent since returning from Circle B with Donna Fleming. She had dreaded letting Banning's old friend and benefactor know of her decision to continue her flight to New York, using money borrowed from Donna Fleming. Instead she had remained a recluse in the privacy of Donna's hotel room.

She waited now until Priggee came up to her, his eyes showing his surprise at finding her here.

"Becky, what's the matter? Why are you in Coulee? Is Banning with you?"

She shook her head, speaking in a barely audible

whisper. "I—I've got to get away as soon as possible, Mr. Priggee. Donna Fleming came out to the ranch and told me that Costaine telegraphed my step-father in Seattle. He'll be here—he may have arrived on this morning's stage."

Priggee waggled his head slowly from side to side.

"You're making a serious mistake, my dear. Does Wes know?"

"He hadn't gotten back from Showalter's ranch when—when I left Circle B. I explained things in a note, along with that newspaper clipping you brought me."

The old man took one of her hands in his.

"What will running away accomplish, Becky? After all, you are Wes's wife. Your step-father can do nothing about that. You're free, white, and of age."

Becky swallowed hard. "I had intended to take today's stage for Wenatchee. Donna loaned me the money to get to New York. She told me the stage left at noon. But she lied. She tricked me. The stage to Wenatchee leaves on Thursdays—"

Priggee felt the hard pounding of the pulse on Becky's wrist. He said in the softest of voices, "Thank God for that, Becky. Go back to Circle B. You belong with Wes Banning."

The girl shook her head. "No. Such a marriage could not work out. Why, he was a total stranger. Wes cannot help but think I'm a common hussy, Mr. Priggee. If he couldn't respect me, how could he learn to love me? He only knew me two days—"

The land agent said in the same gentle, persuasive

voice, "I met my wife at a dance in Hannibal, Missouri. We were married the next day. Out of that union came thirty of the happiest years of my life, and three strong sons and a daughter. There is such a thing as love at first sight, Becky. Believe me."

She lifted her wet eyes to him then, a great relief flowing into her face for him to see.

"I will go back, Mr. Priggee—I will." She tiptoed up to kiss his withered cheek with a fervent gratitude. "Thank you, Mr. Priggee."

The oldster's eyes were suspiciously moist as he whispered, "I'll let you use my saddle horse for the trip, Becky . . . When you see Wes, tell him I want your first baby named for me."

She laughed, a shy note making her voice break. "I'll come for the horse in twenty minutes, Mr. Priggee. Before I leave town I—I want to see Donna Fleming and return her money. And tell her a thing or two besides."

Her being fired with a new zest, the girl tripped up the steps and entered the hotel lobby, intending to leave her bag in the clerk's office while she went down street to Donna Fleming's dressmaking shop.

In the act of entering the lobby she almost collided with Donna Fleming.

"Donna," Becky burst out, "why did you trick me into missing that stage? Are you after that reward my step-father is offering? Is that why you tricked me into leaving Wes?"

She saw Donna's mouth twist into an ugly smile. Reaching into her reticule, Donna brought forth a slip of green paper.

"I already have Mr. Hadley's check, Becky. Did you think I'd let you steal my man so easily?"

Becky dropped her portmanteau, staring past Donna Fleming. Approaching her across the hotel lobby came the tall, domineering figure of Lester Hadley, the step-father who had made her life a hell since the Seattle lawyer had married her widowed mother ten years ago.

Hadley was a distinguished-looking man with a white imperial and Dundrearie whiskers furring his cheeks. His eyes held a cruel glitter as he stepped up beside Donna Fleming.

"Becky, you deserve a whipping," the lawyer whispered angrily. "What will your mother think when she learns you married a common saddle tramp?"

Becky recoiled from the menace in Hadley's eyes. He went on in a ruthless whisper, "We shan't let Halverson know, of course. We'll get this senseless marriage annulled at once—"

He reached out to seize her wrist, but his step-daughter tore free of his clawing hand and spun with the intention of escaping out the door. She found it blocked by Donna Fleming, and without thinking of the spectacle she was giving the other loungers in the hotel lobby, Becky doubled her fist and struck Donna across the mouth with an impact which crushed the girl's lips and drove her sprawling across the threshold.

Becky sensed her step-father's angry lunge from behind and she sidestepped with a deer's cunning and evaded Hadley to race across the Elkhorn's lobby, past the startled negro clerk and on toward the only available exit, the stairs leading to the upper story. Lester Hadley was sprinting after her, slowed down by an arthritic knee, so that Becky had reached the door of Donna's room before the man had covered half the staircase below.

She wrenched at the knob of Room Seven, thinking to gain the balcony outside Donna's room and escape the hotel by way of its outer stairs. But the door was locked and in her panic, Becky fled on down the hall in a blind hope of finding an unlocked room before Hadley could trap her in the corridor's dead end.

The first door she tried opened at once and she flung herself through it before her step-father, bawling her name, clambered in view at the top of the lobby stairs.

This room in which she found herself was the parlor half of a two-room suite identical in floor plan to Donna Fleming's. In order to reach the balcony door Becky had to pass the bedroom entrance, and as she did so she heard a man's voice speak roughly behind the flimsy partition, words which made her forget her need for haste and freeze stock-still:

"Only thing that galls me about leavin' this country is not squarin' my accounts with Wes Banning, sheriff."

A gravelly, somehow familiar voice answered, "Costaine wouldn't have fired you if you'd tallied Banning when you had the chance, Lattimer. Costaine hates a failure. He hates a laughing stock worse, and that's what Banning made of you, strippin' you nekkid and sendin' you home with yore tail between yore legs."

Becky bit her lip to keep from crying out. Lattimer, she recalled, was Butcherblock's foreman; which meant that this room she had blundered into was Greg Costaine's. Lattimer's visitor must be Sheriff Jeffers, Costaine's hired star-toter.

"I'd cash in Banning's chips for him," Lattimer went on, "if it wasn't that Costaine might have tipped off my whereabouts to the Rangers back in Texas. That's the whip Costaine's held over me all these years, knowin' I was on the dodge."

"Where you headin' for, Lattimer?" Sheriff Jeffers drawled.

The ex-foreman of Butcherblock laughed sarcastically. "Think I'd tell you? A hell of a ways from Washington Territory, sheriff. Maybe Argentina. Maybe Alaska. It ain't gettin' fired that galls my hide, Jeff. It's knowin' I ain't got the guts to face Wes Banning and smoke it out with the son."

Becky heard the sheriff's soft laugh. "Costaine's going to take care of your revenge for you, Chet. He's payin' Circle B a little visit tonight, providin' Showalter's outfit moved out today. If you ever come back to Washington, the best you could do would be to spit on Banning's grave. This is one bushwhack deal Costaine aims to handle himself."

Fighting the panic that gripped her being, Becky eased herself out of Costaine's parlor onto the balcony. Leaving the Elkhorn by way of the fire escape, she fled wildly toward Paul Priggee's office.

Her ride to Circle B was something more than a return to her husband. It would be a race to beat Greg

Costaine's ambush bullet. Why Costaine had banished Lattimer forever, she did not understand; but the sheriff's disclosure to Lattimer had been all too clear.

TWENTY-THREE

Wes Banning turned his team around and headed the Conestoga back toward the ranch house when sunset caught him ten miles up the Gap.

He spent this day building fence to keep his and Showalter's cattle from drifting out of the side canyons opening on the North Rim. Day's end found him out of barbed wire, but Big Yak would be back sometime tonight with a buckboard loaded with cedar posts and reels of wire which Banning had sent his Indian to Medicine Lodge to purchase.

He dreaded returning to the Circle B cabin, so filled with memories of Becky's brief tenure there. Jim Showalter and his crew had stayed overnight at Circle B, resting up from the rigors of their trail drive; they had left for their Lazy S round-up this afternoon.

Too restless to stick around the home ranch doing odds and ends of chores until Big Yak got back with the wire and posts from town, Banning had loaded what material he had on hand and had headed up the Gap, intending to build as many canyon fences as possible until his wire ran out.

A full moon silvered the vast reaches of Chinook Gap by the time Banning reached Circle B and unhitched his team. He had turned in a hard day's work and his belly felt empty, but he was in no mood to return to the lonely cabin and rustle himself a snack of bait.

He unhitched the team, turned them into the corral and pumped water into the trough. He could never remember having been more lonely than he was tonight. A coyote was yapping at the moon somewhere out on the Butcherblock flats and he was reminded of how he told Becky not to let the clamor alarm her.

Heading toward the cabin, he found himself wishing that Big Yak was here to join him at supper. Maybe a game of cribbage would take his mind off the emptiness that consumed him. But the Indian would not make it back from town this early. An hour from now, maybe. He would cut some meat from the haunch of venison out in the springhouse and have it cooked by the time Big Yak drove in.

He went to the springhouse for meat and spuds, and with his arms thus loaded down, returned to the cabin, pulled the rawhide latch thong with his teeth and nudged the door open with a boot toe.

The black emptiness of the cabin repelled him. Moonlight pencilling in through the windows picked up a glitter on the dishes and the brass lamp, reminding him of the industrious hands that had polished them.

Banning stepped over to the table and was setting down the venison and the potatoes when the blow caught him from behind, fireworks flashing briefly in his skull before he hit the floor.

. . . He rallied to a dash of cold well water in his face

and opened his eyes to meet the yellow glare of lamp-light on the table beside him.

When he tried to lift a hand to rub the welt on his aching skull, he made the discovery that he was seated in a splitpole chair with his arms trussed behind his back, his legs roped to the chair.

Banning shook his head to clear it. When he opened his eyes again he recognized his own gun belt and holstered Peacemaker resting on the table beside the lamp.

A noise of a water bucket being dropped to the puncheon floor brought his head swiveling around.

Standing between him and the double bunks was the tall, silver-haired figure of Greg Costaine.

The Butcherblock boss was mounting a cheroot under his mustache, the gold caps of his teeth shining malevolently in the lampshine. His black coat was off and he stood there idly snapping the purple garter on his right sleeve, his hooded eyes leveled at his prisoner.

"You kept me waiting quite a spell, Wes," Costaine said, the cigar tip glowing pink to the suction of his draw. "I could have dropped you with my deer rifle as you came tooling that wagon in through the moonlight, but I have a hankering to talk business with you, son."

Banning's jaws grated with muscle. Costaine had been waiting for him beside the door, then, and had felled him with a blow of a gun butt.

"I deserve this, Costaine," the Circle B man said heavily. "I had a hunch you'd let Lattimer handle this."

Costaine shrugged. "My ramrod is in pretty bad shape after that jaunt you put him on. I couldn't wait for him to grow new soles on his feet."

Banning grinned. "Get it over with, Costaine. Even Tex Karnhizel wouldn't draw it out this way."

Costaine strode over to the table and picked up a sheet of paper.

"Unfinished business," the Butcherblock boss said. "You're transferring your lease on the Gap to Butcherblock, for value received. Plus a bill of sale to the cattle Lazy S so handily provided you yesterday. Your John Henry on this instrument will be all my lawyers will need."

Banning was silent for a long moment, wondering if he had any kind of a bargaining lever here.

"If I don't sign?"

Costaine blew a smoke-ring at the lamp.

"You're going to disappear, Banning, just like other small-tally ranchers have disappeared before you. The thing is, you can control the comfort of dying. I've got twelve thousand head of cattle bunched down the creek. I do not propose to drive them to Oregon as you suggested yesterday. I will have the Gap for summer graze even if it entails forging your signature on this release."

Banning tried to steady his thoughts under the hammer blows of his pulse on the welt Costaine's gun butt had raised behind his ear.

"I guess that's how it'll have to be, Costaine," he said. "I sure as hell won't sign your damn paper."

Costaine stepped over to the chair and pressed the tip of his cigar against Banning's cheek bone. The pain of it was excruciating but the Circle B man did not flinch, even when the odor of his own frying skin wafted to his nostrils.

"There's ways of breaking a stubborn bronc like you, Banning," Costaine said, stepping back. "Think it over."

Banning writhed impotently in the ropes which bound him.

"What's the alternative?"

"A quick, clean shot in the brisket."

"How would you explain the blood in the cabin here?"

Costaine laughed. "Who would I have to explain it to? The sheriff? Jeff knows about our little meeting tonight, son. Your Indian roustabout? He won't find much left of this hogan when he gets in from his trip to 'Lodge. You left a fire burning, Wes. A coal popped out. Burned this place to the ground. Regrettable, because Butcherblock could have used it for a line camp cabin."

Costaine stepped over to the table, uncorked an ink bottle and jabbed a pen into it.

"I think you'll sign," the Butcherblock boss said. "Why make it tough for yourself?"

Costaine reached for a stock knife sheathed at his belt, and knelt in front of Banning's chair with the idea of freeing the man's right arm.

As he did so a gust of night wind came into the cabin, stirring the silvery hairs on Costaine's necknape, and making the lamp flame leap on its wick.

"Raise your arms, Mr. Costaine, or I'll shoot you in the back."

136

Banning lifted his head. It was impossible that Becky could be standing there, hair in wild disarray, her bosom heaving with fatigue. She carried a Remington .25-3000 rifle Banning recognized as belonging to his friend Priggee, and there was a rock-steadiness to the muzzle she held at hip level, aimed at Costaine's big shape.

Costaine's eyes held a wild fire in their depths as he came to his feet and turned to face the girl in the doorway, the bowie blade clattering to the floor as he raised his hands.

The girl he had manhandled in Madam Bartreau's took a step into the cabin.

"If you hadn't sent that telegram to Seattle you'd have trapped me here as well as my husband, Costaine," Becky panted hoarsely. "If I hadn't swapped horses at the ferry and Mr. Showalter's ranch I'd never have made it here tonight in time—"

Wes Banning found his voice with an effort.

"Make him step aside so you can pick up his knife, Becky," the Circle B man cried. "Make him turn his back to you so you can lift that .45 out of his holster with the end of your rifle. Don't take any chances on him knocking it out of your hand."

Costaine sidestepped toward the table, carrying out Banning's instructions, and turned his back to the girl. Gripping her Remington in white-knuckled fists, Becky Banning stalked up behind him and reached out her gun barrel to hook in under the curved stock of Costaine's six-shooter.

Before she could flip the .45 out of leather, Banning saw Costaine's body tense and he knew what was coming. What happened next was so smoothly and daringly executed by the desperate rancher that Banning had no chance to shout a warning.

With his left arm Costaine knocked the coal-oil lamp off the table to plunge the room in total darkness. Swiveling with the same movement, his right arm knocked Becky's rifle muzzle away from his body, so that her instinctively jerked trigger drove a bullet into the roof.

Becky felt Costaine's big shape knock her aside as the Butcherblock man bolted through the moonlit door, vanishing instantly.

Banning yelled as he saw Becky pick herself up, levering a fresh cartridge into her .25-3000. She sprang to the door in time to see Costaine dive behind the cover of the granite coaming around the well midway from the house to the barn. Bellied down behind that barrier, Costaine was in a position to shoot down anyone attempting to leave the cabin.

"Cut me loose, Becky!" Banning shouted. "Come in out of his range—"

Even as Becky leaped back into the house Costaine's first shot smashed into the door jamb.

Breathing heavily, Becky snatched up Costaine's knife and came around behind his chair, and he felt the razor-honed blade sawing through his ropes.

"Wes, my darling, my darling—"

He jerked himself free of the ropes and lunged for his six-gun on the table. The room was filled with the rank

138

odor of spilled kerosene and drifting gun fumes.

"Costaine's behind the well," Becky cried out, causing Banning to veer away from the open door and head for the nearest window. "Watch it—watch it—"

"Not now he isn't," Banning ground out. "He's ducked into the barn. Must have his horse there."

He whirled, seeing the dim shape of the girl from the reflected moonlight that penciled through the south window.

"I'll head for the root cellar and try to circle behind the barn," he said crisply. "Stick inside and cover me from the cabin, Becky. If you get a shot at Costaine, fire away. But don't let him spot a hair on your head—"

Banning raced to the other side of the cabin, shoved back the window frame in its greased slides, and straddled the sash to drop to the ground. Six-gun palmed, he raced for the brush-covered hummock of his spring-house, flinging himself in a running dive behind it.

A swift beat of hoofs came down-wind and through the moon glow Banning saw Greg Costaine spurring from behind the barn, mounted on the fleet white Arab.

Rearing to his knees, Banning steadied the Colt barrel across his left forearm, swinging the muzzle to pick up Costaine's big shape in the sights.

It was a moving target but the range was not excessive and a desperate incentive to kill steadied his nerves as he squeezed trigger, feeling the Peacemaker recoil against the crotch of his thumb.

He came to his feet, looking over the grassy mound of the root cellar in time to see Costaine lean back in saddle losing his grip on the Arab's reins. The horse swerved to avoid colliding with a corral fence, and the movement made Costaine's boots leave the stirrups. He cartwheeled from saddle to slam heavily against the pole rails and bounce to the ground, the Arab bolting off into the night with stirrups flapping.

Becky called his name from the cabin but Banning waved her back, recocking his gun and running at a crouch along the corral fence.

Reaching Costaine's sprawled shape, Banning thrust his gun through the waistband of his chaps. His first bullet had drilled Costaine's right temple and had torn out the other half of his skull. This malevolent being who for so long had despoiled Foothill County and dominated its affairs had been reduced between two ticks of a clock to a bleeding hulk of carrion.

He was walking away from the gruesome sight when Becky came to him, limp with reaction and the gruelling toll of this day's ride from Coulee Center.

Banning reached out to pull her into his arms, bending his head to crush his lips demandingly against hers. He felt the wild rioting of his heart as her arms came up behind him, pulling his head down, the swell of her breasts flattening against the hard pressure of his chest.

After a timeless interval he released her. "Becky, now that I got you back, I'll never let you go—"

"Do you love me, Wes? Because I've got to know that—"

"I love you, Becky."

She said with a little child's simplicity, "I am your wife, Wes beloved—to have and to hold till death do us part. That's the way it will always be. Oh, hold me close, Wes . . . I so nearly lost you . . . before I knew you were even mine to grieve . . ."

A rattle of wagon wheels brought them out of their dream and they turned to see Big Yak tooling his wagon team around the corral corner, pulling to a stop alongside Costaine's sprawled corpse.

No change of expression touched the Indian as he shifted his glance from the dead man to the man and woman a few yards away.

"Heap skookum," he said.

Wes Banning said huskily, "Yak, load Costaine into the other wagon and cover him with a tarp for the night." He added something in the Yakima jargon which brought the first grin he had ever seen on the Indian's lips. "When you turn Costaine over to the deputy coroner in Medicine Lodge tomorrow I want you to go around to Sweeney's Furniture Bazaar and bring back that piano he's got for sale. We're going to have music around Circle B from here on out, Yak."

The Indian said, "Chief tell Yak when he young brave, teepee empty without squaw to share blankets. Heap good."

As Wes and Becky started back toward the cabin, closing their minds to the violent events of this hour, the Indian climbed down from his wagon and started to unhitch. He paused in his work to see Banning and his wife reach the slab of pitted lava that formed the doorstep of their honeymoon home.

Across the night Big Yak heard their mingling laughter, and he watched proudly as Banning scooped his bride into his arms and carried her over the threshold, closing the door behind them. It was a tribal rite the palefaces practiced, Big Yak sensed, and it was good.

He led the horses to the barn and when he came back outside he carried a folded canvas in his arms. Before attending to his grisly chore he paused to drink in the beauty of this night, knowing the like of its magic would never come again to the lovers inside the cabin. That magic would grow with the years that stretched ahead.

Overhead a screech-owl winged briefly across the moon. There was something eerie, yet comforting about the remote yammer of coyotes behind the South Rim. A packrat rustled straw in the loft where Big Yak would be making his bed from now on. Somewhere down by the creek he heard a horse nicker plaintively, and knew it was the white Arabian questing its master.

No lights showed inside the windows of the Circle B cabin, and from inside it there came no sound at all.